You

Should have

Listened

When

I told you

The

1st

Time

A Novel by:

La' Kendrick Thompson

March 13th Publishing

LDThompson Publishing Inc.

2305 W Horizon Ridge Pkwy #3123 Henderson, Nevada 89052

Copyright © 2019 *La' Kendrick Thompson*

Printed in the United States of America

Edited by: Melissa Baron

Cover Photo: La' Kendrick Thompson

Cover Design: La' Kendrick Thompson

Author Photo: La' Kendrick Thompson

Authors Info:

Ldthompson81@yahoo.com

Visit the author's website at: amazon.com/author/lakendrickthompson

ISBN: 978-0-578-59848-2

You

Should have

Listened

When

I told you

The

1st

Time

Publisher's Note:

"You should have LISTENED when I told you the 1st time."

This is a work of fiction. It is based on observations, experiences, and opinions from the author's perspective. In no way is the story meant to glorify violence, categorize any specific age group, or to criticize parents. The message is written for the sole purpose of not only highlighting the difficulties that come with parenting and teenage peer pressure, but also the effects of decision making in regards to parent, child relationships.

"Prevention is better than cure."

Desiderius Erasmus

Table of Contents

Part 1

Part 2

Part 3

Part 4

Kelly 2

Elizabeth & John

Perry 2

Mickey 2

Part 5

Omar

Jerome

Brenda

Timmy

Dontae 3

Sharon

Jerome 2

Part 6

Kyla 2

Chloe 3

Jason & Kelly

Riley

Lynn

Jerome 3

Part 1

1

Dontae

The Kankakee High School cafeteria was crowded with teens relieved to get a break from their classes, yet excited to chop it up with their peers. Dontae always looked forward to lunch — not only for the break from class, but also for the school pizza he loved.

After standing in line for ten minutes, he searched for a round table to sit at. One of his longtime friends, Timmy, called his name and waved him over in his direction. Dontae walked over to the crowded table towards the back right corner of the cafeteria, tray in hand, and took a seat. Immediately he became embroiled into a conversation already taking place.

"Donnie. I was just telling Corey you can't go to the party tonight. Please tell this nigga Mom's ain't letting that ride," said Timmy.

Dontae shook his head and looked around the table at the other students waiting on him to respond. "I can go if I want to," he said. "I be chillin though."

Timmy burst out into laughter, and the rest of the table followed. "It's cool if you can't go bro. I'm just messing with you."

"What's your curfew?" Corey asked, stuffing his mouth full with crinkled fries.

"Nine thirty," Timmy replied, clapping his hands and laughing.

Dontae stared across the table at Timmy with fire in his eyes. He was so heated he spoiled his appetite. He couldn't even take a bite of the pizza he'd been looking forward to all day.

"Tim, leave Donnie alone, bruh. Momma just started letting you out the crib," Will said, sensing that his friend was bothered. "He ain't missing nothing."

"Well why you be going nigga?" Corey asked.

"To laugh at ya'll niggas, and to make some money," Will said, pulling a wad of cash out of his pocket and counting it.

The topic of discussion eventually changed, but it didn't ease the pain Dontae felt. Not only was he embarrassed that his bros were baking him like an apple pie, but a girl name Tierra he had a huge crush sat at the table next to him.

And her girlfriends were laughing, too.

She'll never talk to me knowing I have a nine thirty curfew, he thought. He was so mad he wanted to fight, but he did a great job of maintaining his composure.

Besides, Timmy was his homeboy. They always made fun of each other. Only this time it was *his* turn to take the heat, and he hated it.

Dontae's ma was strict and she had a no-nonsense parenting style. At sixteen years old he had a nine thirty curfew, so he'd never attended a party before. She always lectured him about avoiding the traps in the hood, like staying away from his friends, who were known drug dealers and gang members.

But his friends also got to come and go as they pleased. Dontae had never had that kind of freedom, and he was getting tired of the pressure and the shit they gave him for it. He wanted to prove everyone wrong. His mother's curfew was unreasonable at his age, and just…stupid.

Lunch period ended, and everyone headed in different directions to their classes. By the time the bell rang, Dontae had already decided he was going to the juke party. He approached Will in the hallway between classes to talk about it.

"Pick me up tonight bro, I'm going," Dontae said, shaking Will's hand.

Will smirked, but tilted his head up at him in confusion at Dontae's decision. Will was short and light-skinned, with a wavy fade. "Bruh, don't get in trouble trying to prove niggas wrong. It's not that serious."

Dontae looked him in the eye. "Bro, I'm going. Just hit me up."

"Aight, if you say so," Will sighed, shaking his head.

After talking to Will, Dontae went on his way, but stopped in his tracks after hearing a female voice call his name. He turned around and was surprised to see Tierra walking towards him with a couple of her friends. Tierra was a petite, light-skinned girl with Poetic Justice braids and pretty brown eyes.

"You coming to the party tonight, right?" she asked, her eyebrows raised expectantly.

"Yeah, I'll be there," he said, staring at her in amazement.

"Okay, you better come. It's my party and it's at my crib," she said. Tierra gave him a winning smile and left for class.

Dontae walked away thinking, *I gotta go to this party.* There was no way he could miss it. The girl of his dreams was throwing the party and just asked him if he was going. No better way to impress her than to go to the party she was hosting.

Dontae did his daily chores that evening — another rule his mother enforced that he hated. Afterwards, he slouched on the brown leather and cream suede couch in the living room, watching Netflix, checking Snapchat stories, and waiting on a text from his friends.

To his delight, a text notification popped up from Will at 11:00 pm. The text read: *We bout to pull in the alley.*

Dontae turned the TV up and walked to the end of the stairs, peering up to see if Ma's bedroom door was shut. After confirming that her door was closed, he crept out the back door and met his friends in the alley.

When they arrived to Tierra's party, Dontae couldn't believe the amount of people there. Many of his classmates were shocked to see him, too.

"Dontae, what's good bro?"

"Damn Donnie, Mom's finally let you out the crib?"

Despite the extreme amount of paranoia he felt due to his defiance, he accomplished his goal. No longer would anyone be able to say he couldn't stay out late or go to a party. He walked through the crowded shindig with Will, Timmy, and Corey, danced with Tierra, *and* he got her phone number. Will and Timmy acted like getting Tierra's number was a huge accomplishment. They shook his hand, posted on the wall so they could see the entire living room, and congratulated him like they were in the locker room after a football game.

"My nigga," said Timmy, smiling big. "Now you see why we been trying to get you out the crib."

"I know you been tryna to get at her for a minute," Will said.

Corey didn't seem too happy about it, though. He offered up hearsay. "I heard she for everybody, bro."

It didn't bother Dontae. The longer he stayed at the party, the less he thought about breaking curfew and what the consequences could be. He went from checking his cell periodically to see if his mother called or texted to keeping his phone in his pocket.

2

The Rosewood Boys

They pulled into the parking lot of a ten pump Amoco gas station, music blasting and the trunk rattling. The windows were up, and the inside of the black four door '96 Chevy Caprice was foggy and infested with weed smoke. Their heads bobbed as they recited lyrics from Chicago drill music while throwing up gang signs. They were four deep: Will driving, his brother Timmy in the passenger seat, and Dontae in the backseat with Corey. They'd just left Tierra's party.

Will parked the car at pump nine, but not to fill the tank up with gas. Instead, they conjured at the rear of the vehicle, taking pictures with their phones and conversing about the fun time they had at the party. Within ten minutes, the gas station was packed with most of those who lingered — other teens and young adults who'd just left the party.

"Yo that party was lit as fuck," Will crowed.

"On me," Dontae said texting rapidly on his cell.

"I told you nigga. About time Mom's let you off that leash," Timmy said, referring to Dontae as he twisted on his shoulder-length locs.

"Aye keep it one-hunnid, you had to sneak out the crib didn't you?" Corey asked with a grin.

Dontae shook his head. "Ya'll niggas always trying to bake."

"He getting a whooping when he gets home," Will laughed while sitting on the trunk of the car, reading a text.

"Aye, hold up," said Corey. He stretched his skinny, tall form, hand on his corn-rows as he scoped out the scene that caught his attention, his red eyes squinting.

"There go that nigga Perry," he said, poking his chest out. "Ain't that Kyla in the car with him?"

Everyone looked in the same direction. Will hopped off the trunk of the car, joining Corey to get a closer view. He couldn't believe what he'd seen. He tried to pretend like he didn't care, but there was a prick of pain in his heart.

He looked at Perry, a dark-skinned kid with a do-rag covering his fade, sitting in the driver's seat of the car that just pulled into the gas station and talking on his cell…and then at Kyla. He *knew* it was her by the bun on top of her head. Once he made eye contact with her, his eyes widened and his nostrils flared. He felt disrespected and for a moment he was out of touch with reality.

How could she do me like this? How long has this been going on? When he snapped back to reality, he frowned, his lips tightened, and he balled his fist up.

"Damn bro, these ho's ain't loyal," Timmy muttered. He noticed the distraught look on his brother's face, so he put his arm around his shoulders to comfort him. "She ain't have to get you back like that."

Corey shook his head. "Yeah, she bogus as hell for rolling with one of the ops."

"Whatever you wanna do, we riding chief," Dontae said, joining the other three to signify a cohesive unit.

The four teens watched as Kyla walked inside the gas station, looking back in Will's direction as she did.

"Yeah, she know she ain't right bro, that's why she looking back," said Timmy. He gave her the middle finger.

Will's anger continued to build as he stared at Perry like a lion ready to attack its prey.

With no warning he took off and raced towards Perry, who had his back turned while he twisted off the gas cap. Will swung as hard as he could and socked him in the right eye. Perry fell against his SUV.

The other three teens were on him like lions in Will's pride. Perry dropped to the ground and attempted to cover his face as they stomped him repeatedly. The entire crowd at the gas station formed a circle around them to witness the beat down, and many cheered on the violence, some pulling out their cell phones to record it.

And then someone from the crowd screamed, "Here come them boys!"

The crowd dispersed, and everyone scrambled to their vehicles.

3

<u>Kyla</u>

Kyla had bad intentions when she agreed to kick it with Perry. She wanted to get Will back for all the wrong he'd done to her. And there was no better way to get revenge than to kick it with his enemy. She wanted someone, *anyone*, to go back and tell Will they saw her in the passenger seat of Perry's SUV.

She couldn't help but smirk as Perry pulled into the gas station parking lot, knowing someone would see them amongst the huge crowd and then deliver the message for her. Will could suffer just like she had.

When she saw Will's car pull into the gas station, though, her heart dropped like an atomic bomb. "Baby it's too packed here, let's go," she said hurriedly. This was not in the plan. He was not supposed to be here to see her himself.

Anguish flooded her brain when Perry disregarded her words and continued talking on his cell phone. She repeated herself with more force. "P, let's go to the Gas n Wash, it's too many people here."

She did a double take while looking back and forth around the parking lot when she noticed Will staring in her direction.

Damn it.

Her pretty brown eyes, framed by long fake lashes she'd applied earlier to look her best tonight, were wide-open. She'd bitten off much more than she could chew. She opened the door quickly after Perry handed her a hundred-dollar bill, then scurried towards the gas station, looking back every few seconds, worried sick that William would follow her.

While waiting in line to pay, Kyla was as antsy as a kid in a candy store. She kept glancing outside between Will and his crew and Perry. There was one more person standing in front of her, some guy who couldn't remember what pump he was parked at, and it sent her anxiety to the moon. When it was her turn, she slapped the bill on the counter, blurted out "Fifty on pump three," and walked away.

"Ma'am! Your change!" the clerk yelled.

Kyla rushed back to the counter, grabbed the change, and bolted out the door.

The fear of what could happen became a reality when she walked into a crowd of spectators. She couldn't see who was in the middle of the crowd towards the rear of Perry's truck, but she didn't see Will and his crew. She had an inkling of who it was.

When the smoke cleared and everyone scrambled, she raced over to Perry, who was lying on the ground. She helped him to his feet, and they ran to the car as several cops exited their squad cars. Perry drove away, driving erratically. He looked wrecked. One eye closed, a busted lip, scrapes all over his head.

"You knew them niggas was gonna be there," he said furiously.

"What? No, I had no idea P," Kyla pleaded.

They argued until Perry gave up, and then the pair sat in stony silence while he drove. Kyla stayed quiet in the passenger seat, responding to text messages from Will.

That's what we on? He wrote.

Stop texting me, she replied.

Ask your boy how his face feels, Will said.

Block list, she answered.

She put her phone in the front pocket of her light blue ripped jeans as Perry parked the truck in the front of her parent's home. "Lemme know when you make it to the crib," she said as she got out and stood on the sidewalk.

Perry didn't respond. He stared at her, shook his head, and drove away. Kyla watched him leave, worry in her gut as she dreaded what was to come of her actions. She knew she made a huge mistake, but there was nothing she could do to fix it.

4

Perry

Perry had never been this embarrassed before in his life. *Everyone* in the hood saw what happened, and the shame of being battered and bruised in front of his peers, some of which he knew viewed him as untouchable because they damn well better, infuriated him. Everyone knew him and idolized him as if he was a YouTube sensation or an IG celebrity, and he liked it like that.

But after seeing him get his ass beat? He looked weak. Vulnerable. Like Batman without the mask and the cape. Perry didn't feel immortal no more.

He had to send a message. He already decided to retaliate en route to Kyla's crib after checking his cell and getting more pissed at the constant notifications, because he knew it was all about the fight and they'd never let him live it down.

Perry knew where his enemies lived.

He turned on the next block; he was less than two minutes from them. Kankakee was so small that everyone knew everyone — what kind of car they drove, where they lived. Vengeance clouded his mind as he drove east on Court Street and made a right onto Rosewood, a block filled with vacant lots and abandoned houses with black boards covering the windows and doors. The further south he drove on Rosewood, the less abandoned the homes; he passed dark, quiet houses occupied by tenants who were sound asleep in the wee hours of the morning.

Perry slowed his truck down when he hit Will's block. He surveyed the area to see if there was any sign of Will and his crew, but he didn't see the Caprice.

He had a nine-millimeter Beretta laying on his lap.

No gloves. No mask. Just a heart full of rage.

And the rashness of it gave him pause.

His father was in jail, doing life for a murder he committed when Perry was a six-month-old baby. Perry's mother told him all the time how much he looked like his father, or how he was just like his daddy. He could hear her voice as good and evil battled within his conscience.

If you don't slow down you gone end up just like yo daddy.

Perry parked his truck a few houses down on the opposite side of the block, then shut the headlights off to wait in the darkness for the Chevy Caprice to arrive. It was 2:55 am when the vehicle made a right onto Rosewood from River Street.

Perry bit his bottom lip in anticipation. No time for hesitation now. He clutched the handgun in his left palm — he was a southpaw. He lowered the driver's side window and aimed the gun in Will's direction.

Before he could squeeze the trigger, a woman yelled from the front porch of the home he was parked in front of. "Hey! What are you *doing?*"

Perry glanced to his right and made eye contact with the lady. He frantically tossed the gun on the passenger seat, and sped away.

He parked his car in the backyard of his home on Greenwood Avenue, then tucked the gun against his waist before getting out. He watched his back while he power walked towards the house, locking the screen and the top and bottom locks on the back door behind him.

Notifications kept flashing on his phone. He ignored them to peep through the blinds in the living room window, looking for cops who might have tailed him. When the coast was clear, he took a seat on the sofa, remaining in total darkness to check his messages. There was an abundance of calls, text messages, and Facebook notifications.

"Bro I heard you got stomped out."

"Why you let them boys do you like that?"

"We gotta get em."

Not even an hour had gone by and the whole hood knew he got jumped. Several people recorded the fight and posted it on social media, and even tagged him in it. He was fuming. The more he scrolled and read and watched, the more he couldn't handle the comments and the amount of people who shared the recording.

He deactivated his page.

He was so mad that tears stung his eyes, but the humiliation gave him even more motivation to retaliate. He scrolled through his recent calls, tapped the name "O," and waited while the phone rang.

"Yo, I know you heard how the Ops took off on me tonight," Perry said.

"You playing," O replied.

"Nah fam, them niggas snaked me in front of everybody. You know I ain't letting that slide. They posted it on the book and errthang," Perry said, slouched on the sofa.

"We gotta get them goofies."

"For real though, but 5-0 gone expect me to pop em. I need you to lay 'em down for me," Perry said.

"I got you," O replied.

Perry ended his call with O, and a text message immediately came through on his phone from someone named Mick.

He opened the message. It read: *I need one.*

5

Gloria

Gloria woke up, startled from the middle of a bad dream. Someone got shot during her nightmare, but she didn't know who. When the gun went off, she jumped out of the dream and into the dead of night — it seemed so real. She yanked her black sleep mask from her eyes and grabbed her cell phone from the round glass night stand.

The screen on her phone was so bright it made her squint as she checked the time. 2:49 am. Gloria's sleep habits were horrible. She'd be lucky to get five hours on a good night. She climbed out of bed, a leopard print nightgown covering her thick frame, and went to Dontae's room down the hall to check on him. He wasn't there. In the process, she noticed that the TV was still on downstairs.

"Dontae, turn that TV off and go to bed," she called, but there was no response. Gloria walked down the stairs with loud steps to signify her frustrations. She discovered that while the TV was on, all the lights were off, and Dontae was nowhere to be found.

Gloria jumped out of her skin when she heard the loud bass booms of trap music playing outside. She walked out to the porch to investigate. There was a white Cadillac SUV parked in front of her home. A man she didn't know sat inside it, peering across the street.

Definitely suspicious. She'd never seen that car parked on her block before. She yelled out, "Hey! What are you *doing?*"

The SUV sped away. Moments later, she heard laughter from across the street. And she was *very* familiar with one of the voices.

"Dontae, if you don't get yo ass in this house!" she screamed. "It is almost three in the morning."

More laughter followed. She stood on the porch; hands fisted on her hips, and watched Dontae walk across the street with his head down. She met him at the steps and continued her verbiage out of worry and concern for his safety while they walked inside the house.

"So you sneaking out the house now? I can't trust you," she snapped, following him up the steps.

"I was kicking it with the guys and I lost track of time," he explained.

"What time is your curfew?"

"Nine thirty," he answered glumly.

"Right, nine thirty, not three in the damn morning, Dontae. I told you before. You need to stay away from them boys," she said. "I just saw a man parked in front of our house in a white truck, watching their house. They ain't nothing but trouble."

Dontae's eyes got big. He knew who owned a white truck. "Ma, I been knowing them since kindergarten."

"And they been nothing but trouble since kindergarten," she shot back.

Dontae headed towards his bedroom, but Gloria stopped him.

"Uh uh, Dontae, you're grounded. Give me the phone," she said.

"Ma," he responded. "I just got Tierra's phone number tonight and she gonna text me," he pleaded.

"Ma my ass. Give me the phone, and the PS4 controllers. That's a week," she said. "And Tierra, huh? I gave you those condoms for a reason. Always use protection. You don't want to catch something you can't get rid of."

"We didn't do anything. I just got her number," he defended.

"Well you should've thought about that before you disobeyed me," Gloria said, pursing her lips, hand on her hip.

Dontae huffed and puffed after handing her his cell, then shook his head in disappointment.

"We can make it a month if you want to," she said. Her son glared at her, but said nothing and went to his room.

"Lord have mercy," Gloria muttered to herself once he was in bed. Her spirit was shaken. The bad vibes from the nightmare, that truck, and her son missing from the house had her feeling like an evil presence was in her household.

She went back in her bedroom and put Dontae's cell phone in her top drawer. There was a sage bundle on top of a stand in the corner of her room, and she lit it, then blew it out quickly. She cleansed herself, then smudged the bedroom. Afterwards, she walked to the edge of her bed and paused. Gloria dropped to her knees, bowed her head, closed her eyes, and prayed.

Part 2

6

Kelly

Kelly couldn't understand why Chloe hated her so much.

She'd pass her in the halls and Chloe would give her dirty looks. Chloe also made passive aggressive posts about her on social media. Kelly wasn't one hundred percent sure Chloe was sneak-dissing her, but she felt some type of way. She didn't want to unfriend her because she wanted to know what she was saying about her, for the sake of responding on her own posts. It didn't make sense. They'd known each other since kindergarten — there was a time when they were best friends.

After months of speculation, Kelly decided to finally break the ice. Being in the dark was driving her crazy. She wanted to bring the truth to the light, so she sent Chloe a text message.

We need to talk, she wrote.

About what? Chloe asked.

Idk do you have a problem with me? Seems like you're subbing me on Facebook.

Well yea I have a problem with you. You stole my boyfriend you cunt, Chloe wrote.

Really? He came to me. What was I supposed to do? Kelly asked.

Tell him that your friend likes him. Dumb bitch.

Wow you're big mad LOL, Kelly wrote.

You're gonna be mad when I beat your ass, Chloe shot back.

Whateves.

Kelly did know that Chloe liked Jason, but so did *every girl* who went Bradley-Bourbonnais High School. He literally had his pick of the litter. What had Chloe expected?

During the weekend, the tension continued to build on social media, with both girls going back and forth online. Kelly posted a meme that read, *"Hoes be mad when a nigga choose you."*

Chloe would respond with a status like, *"Dumb hoes be happy to be with a nigga that's cheating on them."*

Then Kelly called Jason, screaming and crying into the phone about Chloe's allegations. "You better not be sleeping with that bitch!"

Jason reassured her that she was his only one, and told her to unfriend Chloe. But still...Kelly remained Facebook friends with her. She was too insecure to delete her. Everyone fed into it, instigating the whole mess by offering their two cents and egging the girls on to fight.

It came to a head in the hallway on Monday. Kelly was headed to her locker to switch books for the next class period when she was yanked by the back of her hair and punched in the face.

Her books fell to the floor, along with her phone, cracking the screen. She tried to grab a hold of her attacker, but all she could do was scream curse words at her and beg her to stop. A huge crowd of students watched, some recording and some chanting with each blow to Kelly's face. It was all a blur. She couldn't see who it was until a couple of teachers pulled them apart, but she wasn't surprised to see it was Chloe.

Kelly knew her face was bruised, her right eye would turn black, and a chunk of her hair was missing. The embarrassment of walking to the principal's office afterwards, with many of her classmates watching, whispering, laughing, and pointing fingers, was gut wrenching.

The dean called Kelly's parents after the fight, and that opened up a whole other a can of worms. The principal, however, did not discipline Kelly at all; just advised her to delete Chloe on social media and not feed into anymore of her shenanigans.

Kelly's parents had no idea she was even having issues with Chloe. They demanded that she not only delete her off all of her social media accounts, but that she deactivates her own pages for a while.

That lasted for all of five hours.

Later that evening, Kelly received several text messages and blocked calls from people who were either sending her the fight video, or telling her the video was all over social media. "Damn Kels you took an L," wrote an anonymous texter.

Kelly was so worried and embarrassed over what happened that she couldn't sleep. She couldn't take not knowing what everyone was saying about her, so she reactivated her page and hid her posts from her parents. She unblocked Chloe and added her back on social media.

When she finally saw the aftermath of the fight, she was in total disbelief. The video clip, which only lasted fifty-three seconds, had been shared thousands of times on Facebook. Nearly everyone she followed on IG posted the video in their story or in their feed, and every Snapchat story shared it, too.

The rage she felt inside had her blood boiling like water in a hot tub. Her face was beet red, and buckets of tears poured from her eyes. Against her better judgment, she inboxed Chloe, typing rapidly with both hands, *"I hate you so much. I can't believe you attacked me over a boy. You're trash Chloe and I hope you die."*

Not even a minute later, a Facebook status from Chloe popped up in her newsfeed. It was a screenshot of Kelly's message with the caption, *"I beat her ass and this stalker is still in my inbox talking shit."*

Messaging Chloe only made it worse. Not only did she have to face the embarrassment of the video, but now she had everyone commenting on the status, calling her a stalker and telling her to take her L like a woman. She reported the video, but it was under review.

Fuck my life, she thought. She spent the entire night trying to defend herself from others, or making somber statuses in an attempt to gain sympathy, but no one cared. She was the talk of the school. The joke of the moment.

And everyone had an opinion.

7

<u>Chloe</u>

Chloe and Jason were friends on all of her social media accounts, and they worked together on top of it.

But no matter what she did to grab his attention she was invisible to him. Like some sort of paranormal entity. She'd pay special attention to her makeup on nights they worked together. She'd go to his football games and pretend to be interested even though she no idea what was going on, hoping he'd speak to her anyway. The object of her infatuation was taken, but to her, he wasn't off limits.

After spending the majority of the weekend going back and forth with Kelly about Jason, she came to school with cruel intentions. Jealousy and envy had swallowed her soul in a murky ocean's abyss, and she was ready for the floodgates of hell to open up.

Chloe *knew* that Kelly was the only thing standing between her and Jason being together, and she had to do something to separate them. Not to mention, everyone knew they had beef, so several students had already asked her what she was going to do about it. The pressure of backing up her words was making her sweat. Even worse — she had English class with Kelly first period.

Chloe sat a couple desks over from Kelly towards the back of the classroom, on the opposite end of the door. The classroom was filled with desks that had racks on the bottom for book storage. There were posters on the walls with various grammar rules on them, and a huge chalkboard at the front of the class behind the teacher's desk, where she stood and lectured.

Chloe, however, wasn't focused on the subject matter for the next essay. She looked at Kelly periodically during class, examining her physical features, wondering what Jason saw in her, comparing herself. *Ew, she has freckles. She doesn't wear make-up. I'm prettier than her*, she thought. It bothered her that Kelly paid her no attention at all. She didn't look her way once.

The bell rang and Chloe watched Kelly walk out of the classroom, then followed a few steps behind her. A part of her didn't want a physical altercation, but the hostility and envy had taken over. She'd gone too far and there was no turning back.

Chloe put her phone in the front pocket of her jeans, tossed her books to floor, and grabbed a handful of Kelly's hair. Once she had her head secure, she punched Kelly repeatedly with all her might and yelled obscenities with each blow. She swung harder as Kelly begged her to stop. A teacher had to practically pry her fingers from Kelly's hair, but not without Chloe taking a handful with her.

The teacher picked the petite assailant up in the air and carried her away as she fought to break free for more. "Let me go!" she yelled.

Chloe was forcibly escorted to the dean's office, held firmly by the arm as if she under arrest. The dean called her parents and asked her to tell her side of the story. "She's been bullying me on social media," Chloe claimed. "I was defending myself." Normally she'd face a ten-day suspension, but her parents argued Chloe's point and the suspension only lasted three days.

Worth it.

8

Jason

Jason struggled with depression, but he kept it bottled up inside. He went through life like a walking time-bomb or a shaken-up bottle of Coke...ready to explode as soon as the cap got twisted. During his junior year he lost his mom, Faith, after a long battle with breast cancer. Before she passed, he was a star student and starting quarterback on the BBCHS football team. Scouts from colleges all over the country sat in the stands and marveled at how poised Jason was on the football field. He was ahead of his time.

Then Mom passed.

He took it harder than anyone in his family. His dad, Shaun, was somewhat relieved because he didn't have to watch his wife suffer through chemotherapy and multiple surgeries anymore. Jason's little sister, Kimmy, was eight years old, and although she was hurt, she wasn't able to understand what death meant.

Jason was completely devastated. It felt like his heart had been ripped from his chest. His mom was his biggest fan. She went to all of his football games, even when her health began to fade. She'd sit in the stands, regardless of how bad she felt, determined to support his dreams.

Although it made him extremely emotional to see her in the condition she was in — losing her hair and dropping two pants sizes because she got so thin — witnessing her strength was a huge motivation. Prior to her diagnosis, Faith was a beautiful blonde woman who looked much younger than 52. She'd wear a custom made white and red number seven jersey to his games, with his last name on the back: MORRISON. She would stand and cheer the entire game, and Jason would look over in the stands periodically and smile. He'd run to the stands and kiss her before each game started for good luck. Now that his good luck charm was gone…he could no longer focus on his goals.

Jason's grades fell rapidly. He went from straight A's to a D average. The great poise he once displayed on the field turned into frequent interceptions, quarterback sacks, and fumbles. His life was falling apart, and he couldn't rely on those around him to help fill the emptiness he felt inside.

Jason had been dating Kelly for six months, but she couldn't come close to understanding the pain he was going through. She tried to be there for him, but he kept pushing her away. All of his friends were self-absorbed jocks on the football team who couldn't see past their own selfish existences. Shaun worked a demanding job as a 911 dispatcher for the county. He'd check on Jason throughout the day, but he had to pay the bills and couldn't provide the emotional support Jason needed during the most tumultuous time in his life.

Jason had one uncle that Dad was adamant he stay away from. Uncle Mick was banned from ever visiting their home, and Jason never knew why. For most of his teenage years and up until six months after Faith's death, Jason modeled his father's behavior and kept his distance from Uncle Mickey.

Until, unexpectedly, Mickey showed up to offer his support.

Jason was home alone, craving a soda. He didn't have money, so he unlocked his phone to text Kelly and ask her to bring him a large fountain Pepsi. He tapped her name to open their text message history, but stopped mid text when he remembered he had two dollars in a pair of jeans he wore earlier that week.

He shifted through his laundry basket until he found the dark blue Levi's and dug the balled-up cash out of the right front pocket. After throwing on a pair of gray and white Nike cross trainers and his BBCHS sweat suit, he walked to the nearest gas station. During his walk, he texted Kelly.

I miss you. Are you okay?

She texted him back immediately. *I miss you more, and no. This shit with Chloe is stressing me out.*

Jason apologized for being distant and thanked her for being patient with him.

You're not going to break up with me are you? He asked.

No you idiot. I love you, LOL, she replied. *I literally got my ass kicked for you.*

It took Jason ten minutes to make it to the Speedway on Kennedy Drive. He stopped at the soda machine to the left of the gas station's entrance. He filled the large cup up with ice and placed it under the Pepsi dispenser, holding the button until it filled up.

Then the door opened and his uncle walked into the gas station.

They caught eye contact straightaway. Jason only saw Mickey once that whole year, and that was at his mom's funeral. Mickey wore a black Harley Davidson t-shirt with an old-school chopper on the front, and light blue jeans with holes in the knees. He approached his nephew.

"How's it going, kiddo? I'm sorry about your loss," Mickey said sincerely.

Jason broke down and told him the truth. He said his life would never be the same. Mickey gave Jason his phone number and told him if he ever needed anything to call him. Jason was appreciative, and although he was somewhat apprehensive, this was the kind of support he'd been looking for ever since Mom died. It made him angry with his father. *How can he tell me to stay away from Uncle Mick when he's not there for me?* He thought.

After the quick conversation, he stood in line behind his uncle, sucking the Pepsi through a red plastic straw. Mickey paid for his gas, looking back through the windows at the pumps to see where his car was parked to rattle off the pump number. Jason frowned at the sight of his uncle's arm as he reached out to place a ten-dollar bill on the counter for the gas. The inside of his upper forearm had several marks on it.

On his way out of the store, Mickey observed Jason starting to head back down Kennedy. "Jay!" he called loudly. Jason looked over. Mickey waved him in his direction, so Jason walked over to the pump, still sucking Pepsi out of his straw. "Want a ride?"

Jason wanted to walk, but how could he refuse his uncle's kind gesture? He got in the passenger seat of the car, with his father's warnings speaking to his conscience. *"Stay as far away from him as possible. He is bad news."*

Mickey asked Jason how Kimmy was doing, but before he could reply, there was an incoming call on his cell phone. He looked at the screen and saw "Dad." *Fuck*, he thought, reluctant to answer.

Jason accepted the call. "Hey Dad. How's work?" he asked. The passenger side window was down and there was wind blowing into the phone, which made it clear to Shaun that he wasn't home.

"Hey son. Where ya headed?" Shaun asked.

"I'm on my way home," Jason replied. "I walked to Speedway, ran into Uncle Mick, and he's giving me a lift back home."

Halfway across town, Shaun blew a gasket. He could feel his veins protruding from his temple and his neck.

"Fuck," he said with feeling, shaking his head. "C'mon son, I hope you're just blowing smoke up my ass." He smacked his forehead.

"Dad," said Jason nonchalantly, sipping from his straw as if it wasn't a big deal.

"I told you to stay away from him. He's bad news," Shaun said, rubbing his fingers through his light brown hair. "And I told that mother fucker to stay away from my family."

"I know, Dad, he's just giving me a lift. I'm going home," Jason said.

"Okay, but make this the last ride you take from him. I've already lost your mother. I don't want to lose you, too."

Jason ended the call, and looked at his Uncle Mickey as if he'd taken a ride on the highway to hell with the devil. He took another sip from his straw, and there was an awkward silence between the two. Jason wondered, *what is he doing that is so wrong?*

9

Mickey

Although Mickey couldn't hear what Shaun was saying on the other end of the phone, he knew it wasn't good. He cut his eyes at Jason while driving, sneering when his nephew wasn't looking. A vortex of anger swirled inside him. He shared the same sentiments as Shaun — he *hated* his brother. He despised him for passing judgment and acting like his shit didn't stink. Jason ended the call as Mickey parked his black 4-door Ford pick-up truck in front of his brother's brick home.

"Was that your old man?" he asked as he scratched the side of his beard.

"Yeah, it was," Jason said, unfastening his seatbelt.

"Well. I'm sure he's told you how much he hates my guts," Mick said.

"Yeah, he told me to stay away from you," Jason said with an uncertain smirk. "What's his deal?"

"Childhood BS. He thinks he's better than me. Always has, always will. Oh, and he doesn't agree with my lifestyle," Mickey said, taking a deep breath.

Shaun's disdain for Mickey was deeply rooted in the psychological abuse he suffered during their childhood. Mickey was always the tougher one, so he'd bully Shaun and often attack him physically. Their dad was a marine and Vietnam veteran who didn't tolerate his boys crying, so Shaun couldn't tattle. He'd just tell him to fight back. As a result, Shaun carried his animosity towards Mickey with him into his adulthood.

Mickey's rock star lifestyle only caused him to distance himself even further.

After hearing Mickey's explanation, Jason thought his father's behavior was petty. *Who holds a grudge against their brother?* "Well, that's crazy. Hopefully you guys can work it out. I appreciate the ride, Uncle Mick. I'm gonna head inside," he said.

Mickey watched Jason through the windshield, the wiper blades going back and forth slowly on account of the sprinkling of rain that started up. He hated his brother so much that he wanted to do something to get him back — even if it was as sinister as misleading his son.

Mickey pushed the automatic button to let the driver's side window down, and yelled, "Jay! Come here a second." He watched as Jason walked back out to the truck, then went into the glove-compartment to grab a bottle of pills.

Jason hovered over the window, his hood over his head as the rain continued. "What's up?"

"Say…I know you're probably having trouble sleeping at night since Faith passed. I got some Xannies if you want some. They'll help you rest." Mickey held the orange bottle filled with white pills up so Jason could see.

Jason looked at the bottle. He had never taken Xanax before, but he had friends who popped pills, so he wasn't totally unaware. He knew that Xanax helped with sleep. He also knew that he'd slept like shit since Mom died. Out of nowhere, he heard his dad's voice in the back of his mind yet again. *"Stay away from him. He's bad news."*

"What'll you say?" asked Mickey, green eyes wide-open, eyebrows raised.

"I guess I'll try a couple," Jason said slowly. He reached into the car with his palm open.

Mickey handed him the entire bottle. "You can take them all. I have plenty at home."

"Thanks," Jason said, shocked.

"You have my number, kid. Call me if you need anything."

Mickey drove away with a satisfied smirk. Moments later, his cell phone rang. He looked at the screen, and wasn't shocked to see it was Shaun. He answered and Shaun blurted out, "Stay the hell away from my kid, you junky," then ended the call.

Part 3

10

<u>Corey</u>

Corey was so angry he could kill a brick. The driving force of his anger was fueled by his lack of self-control, and an unwillingness to accept any responsibility for his condition. *Can't believe I let one of these thots burn me,* he thought furiously. He'd just walked out of the restroom after pissing hot coal from his penis. He shook with fury, and tried not to make his emotions noticeable to the hundreds of students walking the hall.

He sat at his open-front desk, trembling with rage, frowning deeply, his close-set eyes squinted and scoping out a couple of girls in the class he'd slept with.

Corey's promiscuity made it difficult to narrow it down to one or two girls. He'd take a swim in any pool that was open, and now he was drowning in shame. The more pain he felt, the more he thought about acts of violence towards whoever infected him.

Corey had no idea what to do or who to talk to about his health. He thought about going to the school clinic, but he was too embarrassed to tell anyone. He couldn't tell his grandma because she'd tell him "I told you so." He could hear her voice in the back of his mind after he bragged to her about all the girls he had.

"Why won't you find you one girl? Fooling round with all these girls ain't good baby."

Ironically, on the same day he started having symptoms like the burning, discharge, stomach cramps, and the sudden urge to pee, he sat in his health class, at a desk next to Dontae, on the brink of tears as the teacher lectured the class on STDs. The more the teacher discussed signs and symptoms, the more anxiety he felt. He couldn't figure out which STD he had: Chlamydia? Gonorrhea? Trichomoniasis? Most of them caused pain upon urination. The thought of having genital herpes made him cringe. *I don't wanna have sores on my penis,* he thought, full of dread. The teacher handed out pamphlets with information on where to go to get treated if they became infected.

"The Kankakee County Health Department will treat teens over sixteen who are having symptoms," she informed them.

I can't go there. Someone I know might be there.

He was antsy and visibly disturbed enough, apparently, for Dontae to whisper, "You okay, bro?"

Corey shook his head no. His eyes followed Tierra as she walked out of the classroom with purpose. He hid his phone under his desk and texted a few of the girls he had sex with in an attempt to gauge who infected him.

Hey what's good?

How you doing

What you been up to

Corey went straight to his grandmas' house on South Rosewood after school, and ran to the restroom to pee yet again. Once again it burned, and he wracked his brain for a solution. He did a Google search on his phone to see how to make the pain go away without going to the hospital. He tried searching for home remedies to cure STDs, but nothing helpful came up. In fact, all the articles he read advised readers to consult with a physician. He was livid... but also coming to the realization that he needed his grandma.

Grandma Shirley Jean had raised him since he was five years old. His ma was sentenced to 25 years in prison for second degree murder after killing her boyfriend's side chick when he was three years old, and he never knew his real dad. His mom's mom took him in and did her best to fill the void in his life, but Corey often felt like an orphan. He had no father figure or positive male role model.

The only other family he had was his big brother Deon, who he witnessed getting murdered a couple of years prior. Deon got in a verbal spat with someone over money and they shot him in the head. The shooting traumatized Corey, scarring him both mentally and emotionally. Watching his brother's blood paint the sidewalk left him paranoid, and he made it his business to carry guns for protection. He firmly believed that if his brother had a gun on him that day, he'd still be alive. It changed his entire outlook on life and put him on the defense. He vowed to protect himself and his loved ones at all costs.

He failed to protect himself from sexually transmitted diseases, however.

The constant bathroom visits and the excruciating pain took its toll on him, so he decided to tell his grandma he was sick...but not exactly *why*. He figured he'd tell her he was having flu-like symptoms and she wouldn't question anything.

"Grandma, I don't feel well," he said, making himself cough.

"What's wrong with you?" she asked.

"I don't know, I feel sick," he replied.

"Okay. Sick how?" she asked, her gray eyebrows raised suspiciously.

"My throat hurts," he answered, reaching for his neck.

"Gargle some warm salt water and take a nap," she advised.

A nap? What the hell is that gonna do? "Grandma, can you just take me to the doctor, please?" he asked.

Shirley Jean looked him upside his head, then walked through the kitchen, sliding her feet in her white house-shoes, her bright flowered house-coat fluttering behind her. She wiped down the counters with a towel. "I'm not taking you nowhere till you tell me what's wrong," she said.

"I told you what's wrong," Corey said, frowning.

Shirley Jean stopped cleaning and pursed her lips. She cut her eyes at Corey, who sat at the kitchen table and avoided eye-contact. *This lil nigga think I'm boo-boo the fool,* she thought.

She walked over to the table and Corey flinched, thinking she was about to hit him, but she placed her hand across his forehead to see if he was warm. "Child, please. Do you think I was born yesterday?" she asked, hand on her hip. "You done let one of them pissy-tail girls give you something?"

Corey began to thumb wrestle, swallowing, then biting his bottom lip.

"You hear me talking to you, boy?" she asked firmly.

Corey shook his head yes, peering down at the table, ashamed of himself. "Yes ma'am," he said.

Shirley shook her head. "Hmm, I told you not to sleep around with all those heffa's," she said, slapping him on the back of his head. "Trying to be a playboy. Now I gotta miss my stories, cuz yo stupid ass need to go to the hospital."

11

Tierra

Tierra sat at her tablet arm school desk, clutching her right side in excruciating pain. Her lower abdomen was sore and there was a sharp aching pain in her stomach. She asked her algebra teacher for a pass, and rushed eagerly through the hall and to the restroom to relieve the intense urge to pee. The pressure on her pelvis caused pain with each step, and after opening the stall door and sitting on the toilet, she found out why. Her insides burned like hot Crisco as her urine dripped in the toilet. She wiped, and looked at the toilet paper. There were streaks of blood on the tissue.

Worry swelled in her throat as she pulled her jeans up and looked down in the toilet. More blood. Her heart dropped, and her face started sweating as she became overwhelmed with fear. She pulled out her cell phone and Google searched, "pelvis pain blood in urine." The first hit was a UTI; common with women, she knew, especially those who drank as much soda as Tierra. The Google search calmed her nerves a bit. For a moment she was afraid she caught an STD because she'd been slept with a couple of different dudes recently.

A text came through on her phone as she exited the restroom. *What's good, you okay?*

The message irritated her, so she didn't respond. She stood at the water fountain and took several gulps before a teacher passed by and asked for her pass. The teacher told her to hurry back to class after she presented the pass, and she did.

Tierra texted her ma when she returned to class to tell her about the pain she was in, and that she thought it was a UTI. Ma told her to drink water, *not* soda, and that she'd pick her up to take her to the doctor.

When Ma took her to the clinic, however, she found out that she didn't have a UTI.

12

Dontae 2

Dontae woke with a sore throat and an excruciating urge to pee. He groaned and grabbed his stomach, where there was an aching pain in his pelvis and lower abdomen. He'd probably held his pee for too long. Dontae got up and went to the bathroom right outside of his bedroom.

His conscience spoke to him as he stood in front of the toilet, and it spoke in his mother's voice. *You need to stop pissing on this toilet seat and lift it when you go.*

Once he lifted the toilet seat, he screamed the second he began to urinate. It was the pain of all pains, a burning sensation he could barely stand. He didn't know why it was happening. Once again, his mother's voice spoke to his conscience.

Make sure you let the toilet seat down after you go.

He slammed the toilet seat down and ran downstairs to the kitchen, then chugged a water bottle down. *Maybe I didn't drink enough water yesterday,* he thought.

Not a minute went by before he had the urge to pee again. He went to the downstairs bathroom this time, afraid to go, hoping he wouldn't feel the same pain again, but he did. With tears in his eyes, he stomped back upstairs to his bedroom and grabbed his cell phone off the night stand, opening his internet browser. Google always had an answer. He typed "burning when I pee" in the search box, and there was a hit from an article stating, "A burning sensation with urination can be caused by infectious (including infections, or STDs such as Chlamydia and gonorrhea) and noninfectious conditions, but it is most commonly due to bacterial infection of the urinary tract affecting the bladder." He tossed his phone on the bed and bawled his eyes out as the urge to pee hit him once again.

He got up to run to the bathroom, but his cell phone rang. He looked and saw Tierra's name on the banner. Dontae unlocked his phone to read the text message. *GM baby. How r u.*

Instant ire, along with regret, immersed his spirit. He chose not to respond to her text, and went to the bathroom, once again feeling the burn. He thought back to the previous week, and he regretted his decisions.

Not long after Dontae sat in health class next to Corey, who had been visibly distraught, the teacher did a lecture on reproduction and how to prevent pregnancy. The teacher showed a video of a mother giving birth, which horrified many of the students.

Dontae didn't pay attention, however. He scrolled through social media the entire class period and was busy texting Tierra, sending messages jokingly about her having his baby someday. When the bell rang, he walked Tierra to her locker, hand in hand.

"I'm thinking about skipping school," she said casually, her books and phone in one hand while Dontae secured the other.

"Why?" he asked.

"I just don't want to be here today. Since I got my car I be dipping out. Plus my ma at work. We can chill and watch Maury," she said, laughing.

"You are NOT the father," Dontae joked. "That show funny as hell."

"You coming or nah," she asked as they went past her locker.

"I guess I am," he said.

They got in Tierra's KIA Sport and drove to her house on Station Street. They watched the show and laughed, paying very little attention to the purpose of the show.

Tierra expected Dontae to make a move, but he didn't. He continued watching, oblivious to her motives. She grabbed the remote off the coffee table and turned the TV off because her patience had grown thin.

"What you doing, they was just about to read the results," said Dontae, turning his head towards her, his locks swinging.

"Let's go upstairs. I want to show you my room," Tierra suggested.

Dontae's heart started racing, and nervousness consumed him. He knew what "show you my room meant." She grabbed him by the hand and led him up the stairs, and he stared at her booty the whole way. Dontae was a virgin, and had absolutely no idea what to do. They sat on her queen-sized bed, and she could see the nervousness in his demeanor.

"Relax. It's going to be okay," she said. She stuck her tongue in his mouth, but he didn't know how to kiss. The more Tierra's attempts to indulge in intercourse with him escalated, the more uncomfortable he became, so he made an excuse to stop.

"I don't have a condom. I was joking about the baby," he said.

She smacked her lips. "Boy, do not play with me. You don't have nothing to worry about. I'm on birth control."

He wanted to stop. As usual, whenever he was about to do something Ma had lectured him about, he heard her voice. *"Always use protection. You don't want to catch something you can't get rid of."*

He didn't listen this time.

Instead, he thought about how bad it would be if anyone found out he was afraid to have sex with her, so he went through with it. Tierra unzipped his jeans and grinded on top of him. The encounter lasted all of two minutes. Afterwards, the two teens talked.

"What if you end up pregnant?" he asked, vexed and paranoid. "I'm not ready to be a dad."

Tierra rolled her eyes. "Boy I told you, I'm on birth control. I take my pills faithfully."

"Well my ma said girls lie about being on birth control all the time, just to trap a nigga," he said.

"What I'm gonna trap you for, Dontae?" she asked, laughing. "You ain't no baller nigga."

They fell asleep in each other's arms, and that quick nap turned into three hours. Tierra was awakened by the sound of her ma calling her name from downstairs.

"Tee," she screamed. "Come here. The school called me today."

Tierra rose quickly from the bed. "Donnie, you gotta get outta here, my ma home," she whispered as she nudged him in the side frantically.

"Your ma home?" he asked, astounded, his eyes widening.

"Yeah nigga, put your clothes on," she said as she locked her bedroom door.

They got dressed as fast as they could, and the sounds of her ma's footsteps grew closer and closer.

"Tierra, do you hear me?" she yelled.

"Yeah, Ma, I'm getting dressed," Tierra yelled back. She pointed Dontae towards the closet. "Get in there," she whispered.

Dontae went inside, and Tierra slid the wooden door shut. Ma twisted the locked knob and knocked on the door repeatedly as Tierra raced around her bed to open it. As soon as she unlocked the door, Ma pushed past her and surveyed the bedroom suspiciously.

"What took you so long to open this door? You need to clean this room. It smells like ass in here." Jasmine was panting from hauling up the stairs. "I'm sick of you skipping school," she said angrily.

"I didn't feel good, Ma. I gotta headache."

"Have you been taking your medication?" she asked.

"Yes, Ma'am," said Tierra, sighing and rolling her eyes.

"Good. I wish you'd listened to me. You dodged a bullet this time. Next time you might not be so lucky."

"Okay, Ma, I don't wanna talk about this right now," Tierra said with frustration.

"I don't give a damn what you want to talk about. And who do you think you talking to? You gone make me knock yo ass to the middle of next week."

Dontae stood in the closet, curious about what medication Tierra's ma was talking about. *Dodged a bullet?* He thought.

When he asked Tierra about it later, she said, "Oh, she talking about my birth control. She so afraid I'm going to get pregnant." Dontae believed her. He snuck out the house after her ma got in the shower, and then walked home.

Now, he was trying to figure out how to break the news to his ma. He had a box full of condoms in his dresser drawer that she bought for him days ago, and he'd have to explain the painful symptoms he was having. He was embarrassed, hurt, angry, and worried all at the same time, but he called her because he didn't know what else to do.

Dontae's ma, Gloria, was a Qualified Intellectual Disability Professional, or QIDP, for Pinnacle Opportunities. She managed a group home built to assist disabled adults with daily living skills in the area. She was sitting in her office, typing an individual service plan for a resident, when Dontae's call came through.

"Boy, what do you want? And yes, you are still grounded."

"Ma, something wrong with me," he said.

"What's wrong now, Dontae," she asked, exhausted with his behavior as of late.

"It hurts when I pee," he groaned.

"Hurt how?" she asked, eyebrows raised, service plan forgotten.

"It burns," he said, breaking into sobs.

Gloria took her phone off speaker and picked it up to put to her ear. She slid back in her chair, away from her desk and laptop. "You've been having unprotected sex, Dontae? Why? I just bought you condoms."

Dontae sat on his bed, speechless because he couldn't tell her why he didn't use protection.

"Now I have to leave work and take you to the clinic," she said.

During the ride to the clinic, she slapped him upside his head and called him stupid.

"You better hope it's something you can get rid of," she warned. "And let me guess, it was Tierra?"

"Yeah," he said, his head down in shame.

"How long have you known Tierra?"

"Since kindergarten," he said.

"See, there goes that kindergarten shit again. How many times has this happened?"

"Just once," he replied, tears in his eyes.

"She could get pregnant, have AIDS or anything. You gotta be smarter than this. I didn't drop you on your head when you were a baby. I don't understand you."

No matter how embarrassed Dontae was to tell his ma he had a STD, he was even more embarrassed when he had to explain the symptoms to the doctor. Doctor Kim, an older white man with gray hair and black eyeglasses, sat in a rolling stool across from the examination table Dontae sat on. He explained what his symptoms were, getting choked up just to have to say them out loud.

Dr. Kim listened, then left the room and came back with a long Q-tip. Dontae blurted out, "What you bout to do with that?"

"I have to take a swab for labs," Dr. Kim explained. "I'm going to open up the head of your penis and stick this inside of it. There's going to be a bit of discomfort, but I need you to be still."

"Ma," cried Dontae.

"You made the bed," she said, shrugging her shoulders, although there was pain in her heart.

Gloria looked away as Dontae lowered his jeans.

The doctor looked at his penis and said, "There is some green discharge."

He stuck the Q-tip inside Dontae's penis, swabbed for the sample, and left the room. Tears flowed down Dontae's cheeks. All he could think of was how much he hated Tierra. *I'm never having sex again,* he thought.

Just when he believed the pain and embarrassment was over, Dr. Kim returned with a needle and a medicine cup containing two pills. Dontae was asked to lower his jeans yet again, and received a shot in his right ass cheek. He took the pills, and the doctor took a few minutes to counsel him.

"The pain should subside immediately, and soon you won't feel any pain at all. Mom, here's a script. Please make sure he takes each and every pill. Dontae, do not engage in any sexual activity until you've taken them all, and son, no matter what…protect yourself at

all times."

Part 4

13

Chloe 2

There was a neighbor game on Twitter, and when Chloe saw the hashtag #numberneighbor on several tweets, she couldn't wait to play.

The object of the game was to replace the last digit in your phone number with the next number up and send a text to that person with a neighborly greeting. Chloe's number ended in 9330, so she contacted an anonymous person whose number ended in 9331.

Hello neighbor, she wrote.

The "neighbor" responded shortly after. *Who's this?*

It's your neighbor, Chloe replied.

My neighbor is an elderly lady who I'm sure knows nothing about texting. Who is this? The neighbor asked again.

Chloe, she said.

The neighbor sent a blank face emoji.

Do you have Twitter? she asked.

The neighbor said no.

Well there's a neighbor game on Twitter, she explained.

The neighbor read the anonymous texter's explanation, and his suspicions grew. He saved Chloe's number and browsed through social media to put a face to the name. On Facebook, a search for that number brought him to a profile for Chloe Truman. Her profile picture was a short-haired blonde bitmoji. He searched

Snapchat and found a user named "chloe_hot1" with the same bitmoji.

The neighbor went back to the text message thread, because Chloe had written him again.

What's your name? She asked.

Mike, he replied.

Hi Mike.

Chloe sat at her desk in class, her cell phone in her lap to hide it from her teacher.

How old are you? Mike asked.

18, Chloe typed, adding an extra two years. Then she texted her friend Riley, who also played the game.

My neighbors a guy named Mike LOL, she wrote.

Lucky you, my neighbor was my mom LOL, said Riley. *Is Mike hot?*

Idk, Chloe answered, *but he doesn't have Twitter.*

He's probably some old creepy guy then…maybe you should stop texting him, Riley reasoned.

Chloe took Riley's advice and ended the conversation. *Nice to meet you neighbor, have a good one,* she wrote.

"*Take Care,* said Mike, and that was that.

14

Fred

Mike's fascination with Chloe grew like a parasite. He viewed her Snapchat stories, since her account was public. He tapped her bitmoji face, which exposed her "Snap Map," and zoomed in to see her exact location. Bradley, Illinois. Hemlock Lane. He grinned slyly. Chloe's Facebook personal information was also public. She went to Bradley Bourbonnais Central High School; her relationship status was single, and she was interested in men. Her photos were public. She worked at Arby's, and her birth date was February 2, 2003.

She lied about her age, he thought. He couldn't get mad about the lie; he lied and told her his name was Mike. His real name was Fred. He just assumed she was into older men, which fascinated him even more at fifty something years old.

He'd driven to Bradley Bourbonnais High three days straight since Chloe sent him a message, hoping to see her. The first two times he was disappointed, but the second time he saw her walk out the school with her books in hand. He vowed to return.

Fred had just ended a call with a customer inquiring about his insurance policy. He looked at the time on his laptop. 2:15 pm. He tapped his fingers on his desk, contemplating whether or not he should take another trip south to lay eyes on Chloe again.

He powered his laptop down, unplugged it, and placed it inside his leather case. He went into his bosses' office, claiming to have a migraine, and took the remainder of the day off.

While walking out of Quality Life, the insurance company he worked at, he wondered if he'd finally get the opportunity to meet Chloe, hoping they'd hit it off and he could finally touch her, kiss her, and possibly have the encounter he assumed she wanted. *She likes older men. And I'm much older than she is.*

He decided to take another look at her Facebook page before driving to meet the object of his obsession. He smiled while looking at the last few statuses she made.

"I need a man who will grab my butt and call me pretty."

"I can be that man for you," he murmured.

"First day back at school after beating Kelly's ass LOL."

"That's why you weren't at school the first time I came," he mused.

He sat in his car in the parking lot and marveled at how beautiful she was in her pictures, then read through the comments guys made and saw how many likes she received. After a few more minutes of cyber stalking, he decided to drive the twenty-five minutes south it would take to meet his "neighbor" once again.

He took Route 50 south, through Manteno, past Bourbonnais, and into Bradley, where he made a right on North Street, heading towards Bradley Bourbonnais High School. With one hand on the steering wheel and the other on his cell phone, he continued to scroll through Chloe's profile pictures, salivating at the mouth like a dog in heat. He crossed a set of train tracks and dropped his speed as he approached the high school, still ogling Chloe's profile picture.

He drove back and forth down North Street several times, frustrated that he could not find her. It had been years since he'd felt this way about a girl, and he refused to give up. He parked his car across the street from the school, and watched like he'd done so often.

Finally, he spotted her walking out the front entrance and down the steps of school. She had a pink and black Nike backpack on her shoulders, and a cell phone in her hand. He pulled off slowly, breaking at the stop sign at the intersection of Cleveland and North Street, watching as Chloe walked east on North. The traffic flow was heavy, with cars moving slowly to obey the school-zone speed limit and stopping to let hordes of kids cross the street. He was relieved to finally make a right turn and spot Chloe, who'd made it further down North Street.

Fred yielded in the turning lane, scowling at the traffic flow in the opposite direction, which was heavily congested with school buses and parents picking up their kids. He bucked his eyes as he was able to get a closer view of her, and admired the petite teen that was still unaware that she was being followed. Fred made a left turn onto Washington as the traffic flow came to a halt from an Amtrak train speeding along the tracks.

He followed her slowly, breaking his neck in her direction and looking in his rearview mirror periodically. His blue minivan passed Chloe, still oblivious and only focused on her phone. She had her ear buds in her ears and her gaze down at her phone while she texted.

Fred made a left on Hemlock Lane and parked the van next to a small park with a paved basketball court. He watched Chloe pull her key out the front pocket of her jeans, and enter her brick home. The house number was 228, and the driveway had no cars. He tapped the home screen on his phone to see what time it was: 3:30 pm. Her parents must be at work.

Chloe was home alone.

15

Kelly 2

Kelly's entire night consisted of browsing social media in an attempt to defend her honor. The self-consciousness she'd already wore on her sleeve increased by thousands as she gave her bullies more ammunition to torment her.

Chloe turned into a local celebrity as the video managed to go viral, and Kelly became the laughing stock of their small town. Her parents didn't have a clue what was going on. She couldn't tell them because they told her to stay off of social-media.

She called Jason, sobbing uncontrollably. "There's no way I'm going to school tomorrow. Do you see this shit?" she asked.

"What are you talking about?" he inquired.

"They're still talking about the fight," she cried.

"Kelly, you need to take a break. It's not going to stop until the next thing comes along," he said, sighing.

"Great, blame me," she said, rubbing her fingers through her hair.

"Not blaming you, but no one is making you read the posts. Look, if you don't want to go, I'll stay home tomorrow. We can ditch together," he offered.

"Okay, "she said, sighing with relief.

"But what are you going to do after that? Skip every day?"

"I know I can't. I just need a day. I've literally been up all night crying," she said.

Despite Jason's advice, Kelly remained on social media. She sprawled across her bed, pulling at the top of her hair with each notification. Her green eyes were bleeding with agony as the deep emotions from within flowed down her face like a river dam.

There was no way in hell she was going to school the next day to face them. No one seemed to care if she felt victimized, not even her boyfriend, who was the main reason she was suffering to begin with. She was being used as a human punching bag, and she hated it. She tried to sleep, but every time she closed her eyes she had visions of walking through the hallways and the entire school — her classmates and her teachers — all pointing fingers and laughing at her hysterically.

Kelly followed her daily school day routine: hair, clothes, make-up, and peanut butter toast to go. Instead of walking to school, though, she walked to Jason's house. When she arrived, they hugged in the doorway, and Kelly buried her head in his chest, which made her feel safe.

He kissed her on the forehead and said, "My dad is working overtime this morning. And give me the phone. No social media. You're going to get some rest."

Kelly handed him her phone and they cuddled up in his bed, but her mind couldn't rest. She was still worried about what people were saying, and the fact that she didn't have her phone to see it all was driving her crazy.

"Kels, you need to get some sleep," he insisted, lying on his side. He hadn't changed out of his wife beater and red pajama pants sleepwear.

"I'm trying, but I can't," she said, sitting up in the bed. She was still fully dressed in a red Tommy H shirt, dark blue matching jeans, and tweety-bird socks.

"Look. My uncle Mickey gave me some Xanax yesterday to help me sleep, and it actually helped. I haven't slept that good in months," he said. "Want one?"

"Xanax?" she asked, eyebrows raised. "I don't know. I hate pills." But the more exhausted she grew by the minute, the more appealing it sounded. One couldn't hurt, right? Doctors prescribed it all the time. "I mean, why not? At this point I want to slit my wrists and end it all."

Jason grabbed the bottle off his night stand, screwed the white cap off, and dumped one pill in the palm of her hand. He gave her water from the water bottle on the night stand. Kelly gulped the pill down quickly, and within fifteen minutes, she was sound asleep.

16

Elizabeth & John

Elizabeth and John sat at their kitchen table conversing while she prepared dinner: steak, baked potatoes, and asparagus. They were an old school couple. John had brown hair, blue eyes, and was muscular for his age. He'd been a firefighter for Bourbonnais for the last fifteen years.

Elizabeth, a short, slender woman with a cap of red hair and freckles, was a stay at home wife who took pride in the upkeep of their home and taking care of their daughter. John still read the newspaper every day after work, and Liz enjoyed offering her opinion on different columns or articles within their favorite sections: the front page, the local news, and the blotter. On the front page was a story with a shocking headline: "Former area star athlete found dead of heroin overdose." The middle-aged man had been found dead in his apartment with a belt tied around his arm.

"I remember him from high school," Liz said, shaking her head in disbelief. "I don't understand what drives people to do drugs."

"Could be multiple things," John replied. "Depression, job stress, addiction that may have started at a very young age…it's scary. I've arrived on many scenes where even kids have overdosed."

"My God. I don't know what I'd do if that happened to Kelly," Liz said, taking a sip of tea.

"Kelly's too smart for that," John replied. "She knows better."

Moments later, Kelly walked through the door with her backpack slung over her shoulder, wireless ear buds in her ear, and her phone in hand. She greeted her parents with a kiss, then headed for her bedroom to check her text messages.

"Sweetheart, come sit down with your mom and me, "John called in his deep, booming voice.

"Dad, is this about to be one of those talks? I have a test in biology tomorrow. I need to study." Kelly sounded, and looked, tired.

"Kelly Jean," Liz reprimanded, her mouth open.

"This won't take long, Princess." John folded the newspaper and placed it on the table. "How was school?"

"It was okay," she said with a straight face.

"Okay." His eyes squinted. "I hope you'd tell us if you're being bullied."

"Well I'm not being bullied, so there is nothing to tell," she said.

"Good," Liz said. "We were worried, and that's why we wanted you to stay off of social media for a bit. We know how kids are these days, and we don't want you to harm yourself because you're being bullied," she added, placing her hand on Kelly's shoulder.

"Well I haven't been online, so I don't know what people are saying" she fibbed. Kelly tapped her fingers on the wooden dining table impatiently, and then sighed with attitude. "Anything else?"

"Actually, yes," her dad said. "This may seem like a weird question, but are any of your friends on heroin?"

"Umm no," she said, frowning. "And I don't know if I have any friends right now."

"What about Riley?" Liz asked, as she got up to open the oven and check the food.

"Riley's not on heroin, Mom, and I'm not stupid enough to do drugs," Kelly defended.

"We know you're not stupid, Kelly. We are your parents and we just want to make sure you stay on the right track," Liz said, adjusting her light green apron.

"Anything *else*?" Kelly asked with an eyeroll. John pursed his lips and shook his head no. Elizabeth looked at him, her eyes wide, expecting him to say something, but he picked up his newspaper and continued reading.

17

Perry

Perry returned home from picking up a key of heroin from his connect. His connect said it was the best work on the street, and the junkies were going crazy over it. Perry wasn't satisfied with just having the best product on the streets, though.

He wanted to eliminate all the competition by becoming the biggest drug dealer in *town*. So what if wanting money and a celebrity-like lifestyle made him selfish? He decided to lace the heroin, potent enough on its own, sure, with fentanyl, a synthetic opioid. He read the Kankakee Daily Journal every day. There were several stories about heroin overdoses, some of which he knew he was partly responsible for, and it made him paranoid. However, his clientele was aware as well. Everyone wanted to test the supply that caused other users to overdose because it had to be the best right?

Perry still lived with his mother, Regina, in the basement. He also conducted business down there. Regina knew what Perry was doing, and although she told him how wrong it was, she didn't have the heart to kick him out and he knew it.

He sat on the sofa, with a Chris Rock stand-up comedy show playing on Netflix as he checked his phone periodically. He laughed out loud at the cop jokes Chris was telling when a text came through from Mick.

I'm outside.

Perry rose to his feet and stepped on a stool to loosen one of the basement ceiling tiles. He eagerly grabbed a bag of heroin from the stash-spot just inside the drop ceiling, and then replaced the tile. He walked out the backdoor and spotted the black Ford truck with two white male occupants inside. He kept his palms closed.

He knew who the driver was — Mickey — and Mickey was a loyal customer, but he had no idea who the passenger was. Immediately he thought, *it's a set-up.* He stopped half way; about ten feet in front of the one-car garage, and waved his hand for Mickey to come to him. Mickey, a big dude with a thick mustache and beard, sharp green eyes, and a head of curly brown hair, walked to the garage.

"Who that?" asked Perry suspiciously.

"That's my nephew, Jason," he answered.

"He get high, too?" asked Perry, observing the scraggly blonde-haired teen.

"He wants to try it. You said if I know anyone, send them your way," Mickey said.

Perry frowned. "Damn. Your own nephew, though?"

"The kid has a mind of his own, ya know," said Mickey with a shrug. "These kids love to get high."

Perry squinted his eyes at Mickey and shook his head. The two men shook hands, and Perry put the baggie in Mickey's palm as Mickey put the cash in Perry's palm simultaneously. He looked over Mickey's shoulder at Jason again, then stopped Mickey before he could walk away. "How old is dude?"

Mickey turned his head back, looked at Jason, and said, "Seventeen, eighteen maybe."

18

Mickey 2

Mickey got back in the truck with Jason. The kid had called him thirty minutes prior as Mickey was headed for Perry's house, inquiring about more Xanax.

"Did he have any?" Jason asked.

"No, but I got something better," Mickey said.

"What. Did you get some Percocet's?" asked Jason.

"Even better." Mickey opened his palm to show Jason the baggie.

"What in the hell is that?" Jason asked.

"Fentanyl," said Mickey, laughing. "I mean you can keep popping those pills, but if you really wanna take the edge off, this will put you on cloud nine. It's better than sex."

Jason had never heard of Fentanyl. He stared out the window, contemplating what to do. He was uncertain.

"Well, just try it once. If you don't like it you can go back to taking the pills."

Jason dropped his head and took a deep breath. "Better than sex, huh?"

Mickey smiled big, exposing his chipped front tooth. Jason agonized over the decision while his uncle parked the car at Bird's Park, by the Kankakee River. He was suffering, and he wanted the pain to stop. For a few weeks the Xanax helped him sleep, sure, but it didn't make the grief and stress go away. He just needed a cure.

And Mickey was well on his way to accomplishing his goal of exacting revenge on Shaun.

Jason watched Mickey prep the drug. Spoon. Needle. Lighter. Belt. He tied the belt around Jason's arm after filling the needle, and told him to make a fist. Veins protruded from his muscular forearm. He tensed with anticipation, and Mickey stuck the needle in him.

Jason went into a daze instantaneously and slumped in the passenger seat.

"I bet those Xannies never made you feel that good," Mickey said.

Part 5

19

Omar

At nine pm on a Friday evening, Omar stood in the doorway of his mother's Section 8 two-bedroom brick home, gazing out the screen door at Jerome. The front door was open, but the screen door was shut to take advantage of the slight breeze.

Omar's ma, Brenda, was passed out drunk on the blue contemporary box sofa, an empty pint of Hennessy VSOP on the rustic oak coffee table. The night was silent, outside of Brenda's loud snores and the noise of cars passing by on Station Street. Omar recalled a conversation he had with Jerome two weeks before while sitting on the wide steps of the open porch across the street.

"I got my acceptance letter today," Jerome said.

"Yeah? To what college?" Omar asked.

"Harvard Law," Jerome smiled. "I'm about to be the next Barack."

"Damn. Harvard?" asked Omar, eyes wide in astonishment. "That's what's up."

"Yeah, I'm shocked, too," Jerome said, grinning.

"Wow, niggas from the hood barely go to *any* college and you about to go to Harvard," Omar replied. "Much better than where I'm headed...probably dead or in jail."

His words pierced Jerome in the chest and made him feel bad for bringing up his good news.

"Come back to school, bro, you still got time to graduate," Jerome advised.

Omar dropped his head in shame. "I'll have to go to school next year to graduate. I don't have enough credits. But if I graduate, then what?"

Jerome shook his head, his 360-degree waves spinning, and sighed. He couldn't understand why Omar, who used to be a straight A student, chose another path. "You gotta think positive bro, you trippin."

"Psshh, you don't get it. I'm proud of you though." Omar rose to his feet, his sweat pants sagging, his black Nike flip-flops worn over white socks shuffling against the wood.

They shook hands and pulled each other close for a half hug. "Don't forget about us small people when you blow up," said Omar, grinning, and walked down the steps towards the curbside.

He looked back at Jerome and his heart ached. Despite his troubles, he was happy for his friend, but hearing the good news was just a reminder of how bad his life was. He stared at his house and thought about the times he rushed out the door to the bus stop. He couldn't wait to get to school to have a decent meal, because Ma sold all the stamps on her EBT card for alcohol.

His moment of recollection was interrupted by Jerome, who stopped him as he waited on a car to pass before crossing the street. "Aye, Mom's working midnights now, so I'm throwing a party to celebrate on Saturday. Come through and show love," said Jerome.

"Say no more," Omar replied.

Jerome watched his one-time best friend cross the street, and he was overwhelmed with sadness. He wanted to help him, but he didn't know how to save him from himself.

After his emotional flashback, Omar's phone rang. On the other end of the phone was Perry.

"Yo tonight's the night. I need you to handle that biness for me fam," Perry said.

The eager Omar was more than ready to prove himself. He had nothing to lose.

"I got you," Omar said.

"My hitta," Perry said approvingly. "You know where them niggas be at right? Go through there, air em out, and get rid of the heat. You get picked up you don't know me."

"Bet." Omar ended the call.

Perry was no stranger to beef, and it wasn't his first time having a physical encounter with Will. Omar was well aware of who Will was. He didn't have a personal beef with him, but what took place that night at the Amoco gas station made everyone involved a target. It was his responsibility to retaliate.

Omar had no father figure, so in a strange way Perry provided him with a sense of direction. Perry was one of the few signs of success he'd seen in the hood, even though the fruits of his labor came from drug dealing, robbing, and sometimes killing. Perry had the money, the nice cars, the jewelry, and the prettiest girls from around the way. The ladies loved him and the guys either hated him or wanted to be like him.

Omar had never committed the act he was being asked to carry out, but he had to prove his loyalty to the gang he felt was loyal to him. He walked back to his bedroom, but stopped on the way and stared at his ma, who was still passed out drunk. He looked at the coffee table and cut his eyes to the ashtray full of cigarette butts and the empty bottle of Hennessy. All of it sparked his temper.

He wished things were different. He longed for a loving relationship with his mother, but she was lost. He walked back to his bedroom, opened the top underwear and sock drawer of his oak dresser with the missing handles, and grabbed a black 9mm handgun. He tossed the gun on his twin mattress, grabbed his black hoodie and black jeans out of the closet, and rolled his ski-mask on top of his miniature dread-locs. He bent over to tie his black Air Max runners, stuffed the gun in his black Levi's, and headed towards the front door.

Only to have his mission interrupted.

Ma rose suddenly from the couch, frustration clear on her face. Her speech slurred when she demanded, "Boy get back in your room! Where you think you going this time of night? You ain't got no business going out this late."

"Whatever," Omar replied, smacking his lips and slamming the door behind him.

Brenda flinched as the door slammed, her mind still foggy from the alcohol. But some instinct made her race to the door to stop him. "Boy, who you think you talking to? Omar, you heard me! You don't need to be out this time of night," she pleaded.

He ignored her cries and continued walking, his hoodie on his head to absorb the raindrops that had begun to fall. He checked the time on his phone: 9:45 pm. He continued his stroll down South Greenwood with his arms inside the front pocket of his hoodie.

The further he went, the more he began to second guess himself, but he was determined to follow through on his promise to Perry. He crept through an alley way on Rosewood, took his hoodie off, and pulled the black ski-mask over his face. He walked alongside one of the homes and watched as Timmy parked the black '96 Caprice in front of a house across the street.

His heart beat rapidly, and his arm shook nervously as second thoughts plagued him. He watched as the front door of the home opened.

Will walked out.

Omar fought through his fear, held the gun tightly, and squeezed the trigger sixteen times.

He fired ten shots into the car and six at Will, who dove down on the porch. Omar took off running, dropping his phone, and sprinted up the alley with the smoking hot pistol in the palm of his hand. He navigated through several other alleys, breathing harshly behind the ski mask still covering his face, until he found himself behind Jerome's duplex on the 400 block of Greenwood.

He stuffed the gun inside a trash can, folded the mask on top of his head, and walked calmly across the street with his arms inside the front pocket of his hoodie, struggling to control his breathing. When he approached the front door, he went in his pocket to text Perry.

But his phone was missing. Damn.

20

Jerome

Jerome sat on the porch and observed Omar and Brenda exchanging words from across the street. He went inside the house at 9:47 pm, and locked both the top and bottom locks behind him. He followed his daily routine of prepping himself for bed. He put his wave grease on, brushed his hair in the mirror, and tied his black do-rag around his head. He brushed his teeth with Crest Tarter Prevention, gargled with green minty Crest mouthwash, spit it out in the sink, and rinsed his mouth. He undressed down to his blue boxer shorts, climbed in bed, and put his ear buds in his ear. His ma sent him a text at 9:56 that read: *Goodnight baby. I am so proud of you.*

Good night Ma. It's all because of you, he replied.

He closed his eyes at approximately 10:10 pm, and finally dozed off to an episode of Martin, when he heard the gun shots.

Jerome rose from his bed quickly, panting, and turned his head in the same direction he heard the shots. After calming himself and wiping the sweat from his forehead, he peeped through the blinds out his bedroom window, next to his bed. His eyes widened as he watched Omar cut through the empty lot next to his home and walk briskly across the street, watching his back.

It hadn't dawned upon Jerome that Omar was involved in the shooting. He thought Omar heard the shots and was trying to hurry inside his house.

Nevertheless, he wanted to make sure his friend was

okay, so he sent him a text. *You hear those shots? Wyd?*

Omar did not reply.

21

Brenda

Brenda went back inside the house, feeling less than a woman after Omar showed her absolutely no respect. She thought about taking another drink to deal with the stress, but something in her mind clicked. She was angry...but not with Omar. She was mad at herself.

She walked to the kitchen and grabbed all the alcohol she had in the cabinets and the refrigerator and started pouring it down the drain until there was nothing left. She went to the bathroom and stared at herself in the mirror, with her uneven dark brown hair in a wild halo all over her head, and she was disappointed with how she looked.

"You gotta get yourself together, girl," she said to her reflection. She turned on the shower and shut the door so the steam could fill the room. Brenda stood directly under the showerhead and cried as if the warm water was cleansing her soul. The more she thought, the weaker her knees became. She sat in the tub, cradling herself in the fetal position, crying and shaking as her mind wandered back in time.

Twenty some odd years prior to the night Omar ran through the alleys on the Southside of Kankakee, fifteen-year-old Brenda Evans was awakened by her biracial, 6'3", 260-pound stepfather, Fred, banging on her locked bedroom door in a drunken rage.

"Peaches get up and open this door right now," he yelled.

His demands startled the sleeping beauty, causing her to sit up in the bed. She cried silent tears of fear. Her stepfather continued to twist the doorknob and bang on the door simultaneously.

"Will you open up the door, I just want to talk to you," he pleaded.

Then, without warning, the madness stopped. No pounding. No pleading. Maybe he gave up. That calmed her fears. Brenda wiped away her tears…but her moment of relief was short lived.

Her stepfather stood outside the door with a butter knife, sticking it between the doorframe and the latch until the door popped open.

"No, please don't!" she begged.

That was one of the many nights he raped Brenda, but after that particular night, she vowed it would be the last. For months she was afraid to tell her mother, because her stepfather said he would kill them both.

When her mother arrived home from her shift the next morning, Brenda finally built up enough courage to expose her rapist.

She did not get the reaction she thought she would.

Her stepfather denied everything, and her mother blamed *her*. "You just don't like him. Stop making up lies. He's my husband and you will respect him," her mother said.

Brenda ran away that night, sixteen years old…and pregnant by her mother's husband.

Her moment of recollection was interrupted by the sounds of gunfire, which caused her to snap back to reality. Her first thought was, *my baby*. She shut the water off, wrapped a purple towel around her, tucked it in the front, and walked briskly to the front door.

Brenda peeped through the curtains and was relieved to see Omar hurrying through the yard across the street in her direction. She opened the door.

"Are you okay? I just heard gunshots," she said as he made his way up the path.

"Yeah, I'm good. I heard them too," he answered, with a lump in his throat.

"See, that's why I don't want you outside at night."

He walked past her as if she wasn't there, but she followed him to the kitchen. Immediately he noticed all the empty bottles of alcohol on the counter. "Why are all these bottles everywhere?" he asked as he opened the refrigerator. "You keeping souvenirs now?" he smirked.

She walked up behind him as he grabbed a pitcher of grape Kool-Aid and sat it on the counter next to an empty bottle of Captain Morgan. She started to speak, but she heard sirens howling and saw lights flashing in the darkness. An eerie feeling started weighing on her heart, but she refocused her attention back to Omar.

"Baby...there's something I gotta tell you. Something that's been haunting me all my life," she said. Brenda took a deep breath. "It started when I was fourteen years old. My stepfather, Fredrick, used to rape me. For two years. It messed me up pretty bad." She started to cry.

Omar leaned with his back against the counter, his arms folded. He was in a state of complete shock, and her words rendered him speechless.

"Now I know I've been a horrible mother and I'm not making any excuses for my actions, but...I had a very rough childhood. I told my ma what was going on and she didn't believe me. She took his side, so I ran away from home at sixteen years old. A few weeks later, I found out I was pregnant with you. And that's why you've never met your father."

Omar's eyes filled with tears. He grabbed his mother and held her in his arms as she cried on his shoulder.

"I'm sorry, baby," she said. "I promise I'm gonna do better."

"Me too," he cried, guilt heavy in his heart. "I'm going back to school Monday."

"Good. You're *smart*. I want to see you succeed in life. You gotta stay out these streets. It's only two places you'll end up — either dead or in jail," she said.

"I know, Ma. I'm gonna do better."

Brenda was relieved to finally tell someone a secret she had kept for over twenty years.

And for the first time, Omar felt close to her.

22

Timmy

Timmy left the Phillips 66 gas station on River Street at approximately 9:59 pm. He gazed at the traffic in front of him, the windshield wipers swiping back and forth as the rain picked up on the forty-degree, chilly spring night.

He scrolled through his text messages as he drove, swerved while trying to type, and almost hit a car after driving through a red light at the intersection of South Indiana. He'd just gassed up Will's Caprice and was headed back to their house on Evergreen. They'd worked hard all week selling drugs and recording their new mixtape, titled "Blood Brothers," so they decided to have a little fun that evening. They'd spent the afternoon together. They went to the barbershop on South Schuyler and to River Oaks Mall for new outfits. Timmy wore a new a white t-shirt with a gold chain and a Jesus medallion on his neck. His black True Religion jeans had white thread in the seams, and the new white Jordan 4's had just been released that same day.

Timmy continued texting and driving the entire drive home. He sent Will a text saying *I'm outside* after parking the tinted vehicle in front of their house. After hitting send, his phone started ringing. He held it in his hands and saw "Donnie" across the screen.

He turned his head and looked across the street at Dontae's house, then sent the call to voicemail. Immediately his phone buzzed with the new message. As soon as Will walked out, he remembered how thirsty he was. He forgot to grab something to drink at the gas station.

Timmy hit the automatic switch to let the passenger side window down to ask his brother to grab a bottle of water out the fridge, but a multitude of gunshots rang out before he could open his mouth. Timmy's heart was filled with worry and fear as he looked around, unable to see where the shots came from in the darkness.

He took his seatbelt off and tried to open the door, but the first shot hit him in his left hand. He tried to duck in the car, but he was hit with several shots.

One in his shoulder.

One in his left side.

Two to the head.

Timmy's mouth filled with blood. He strained to breathe as he fought for his life. He could feel death growing near as his heart rate dropped. He gurgled and spit up blood on his shirt. Thoughts of regret crossed his mind in the final moments of his life.

At one time, he had been the star athlete of the area. He excelled at everything: basketball, football, and track, but he looked up to his older brother, William, the most. Timmy wanted to follow in his footsteps, so he focused less on sports, more on selling drugs and becoming a rapper. Their mother felt like Will was a lost cause. His dad was a drug dealer and a convicted murderer, and he did everything his father had done in the past despite never meeting him.

Timmy was the kid she felt had a chance, despite the environment he was in. So when she found crack cocaine and a shoe box full of money stashed under his bed, she tried to intervene quickly. "Baby, we may not have it all, but when you go to the pros, we're *going* to have it all," she said. "This is not you. You're not a thug." She tried to warn him about the dangers of the street life, but he didn't listen.

Timmy took his last breath, wishing he took his mother's advice. But it was too late.

23

Dontae 3

Dontae stood in front of the toilet, urinating in the downstairs bathroom with the lights off. The bathroom was small. There was no tub; just a shower and a sink with a window facing the alley. He zipped his blue jeans up when he was done, then peeped through the white blinds after hearing footsteps in the alley. It was dark outside, with a heavy rainfall, but he was able to identify a familiar face. It was a face he'd seen throughout his entire childhood.

Omar.

He had no idea why he was in the alley, but the longer he stood there, the more curious Dontae became, anticipating Omar's next move. He squinted as Omar paused and pulled a black ski-mask over his face. Dontae's eyes widened rapidly with fear as Omar drew a large black gun from his waist.

Omar walked briskly along the side of the house, so Dontae followed him, looking out the windows in the dining room. All of a sudden, what was going on clicked in his mind. He pulled out his cell and called Timmy's phone, but he got no answer. He called Will's phone, but his voicemail picked up, too.

He raced to the front door and peeped through the curtains as the lights on Will's black Caprice turned off. He opened up his text messages hastily in an attempt to message Will, who he believed was in the car, but he was stunned by several gunshots.

It sounded like midnight on New Year's Day.

Dontae dove to the floor and covered his head. "Momma!" he yelled.

Ma's bedroom door burst open and she came running down the stairs. "Donnie!" she yelled. The gunfire stopped, but they could hear Will screaming from across the street.

"Timmy," he cried. Dontae flung open the front door and raced down the steps.

"Boy, are you crazy? What are you doing!" Gloria yelled, clutching the front of her housecoat and huddling against the door.

Dontae made it to the driver's side of the car, which was riddled with bullet holes, and gazed at his friend's lifeless body. Blood drenched Timmy's white t-shirt.

Will ran towards the car, but turned to hold his ma back in an attempt to spare her the pain of seeing her youngest son's dead body. Sharon fought through his attempt to hold her back and climbed inside the vehicle. William met Dontae at the driver's side.

"Call an ambulance," Will demanded.

"I know, I know who did this," Dontae stuttered.

"Dial 911 nigga!" Will yelled.

Will opened the driver's side door, and wrapped his arms around his brother and his ma. Dontae pulled out his phone and dialed 911 as his ma stood on the porch, tears pouring from her eyes, her mouth covered.

Several other residents on the block stood outside as well — on their porches, in the street, and on the sidewalk, spectating.

"My friend has been shot. Please hurry," Dontae cried. The dispatcher sent emergency personnel immediately, but kept Dontae on the phone for further questioning.

Less than five minutes later, the block was filled with detectives, police officers putting yellow tape around the scene, and emergency medical units. The paramedics took Timothy out of the vehicle and onto a stretcher, and started doing chest compressions vigorously. Moments later, the ambulance drove away with Timmy and Gloria riding in the back with him. The detectives combed the area, looking for clues…searching for answers.

They spoke with Will first. Detective Shaffer asked, "Do you know who would want to hurt your brother?"

Will replied, "No, I don't. He didn't have beef with no one."

They spoke with many of the neighbors who were outside, and no one saw the shooter. When they spoke to Dontae, he failed to tell them about Omar. "No, I just heard gunshots and when they stopped, I came outside," he said.

The detective was pissed, assuming Dontae was lying. "We are gonna keep an eye on this location," he said to his partner. "Someone saw something."

"Snitches get stitches," said his partner.

Will hopped in his ma's black Dodge Journey and drove to the hospital. Dontae went in the house with his ma, who was visibly shaken.

"We need to move," she said. "That poor woman. I couldn't imagine how she feels finding her baby shot up like that," she cried. "This is why I don't like you in these streets, Donnie. That's what I'm afraid of."

Dontae was speechless. He sat next to his mom on the sofa. "Are you okay baby?" she asked, grabbing ahold of him, squeezing him tightly. He shook his head yes, but he was shell shocked, an instant victim of post-traumatic stress disorder. He'd just witnessed one of his closest friends get murdered, and he was in disbelief. Visions of Timmy slumped in the seat, soaked in blood, kept running through his mind. He rose from the couch and walked towards the stairs to go to his bedroom.

"Make sure the door is locked, top and bottom locks," she said. "The back door, too."

Dontae locked the front door first, and walked through the living room, dining room, into the kitchen and locked the back door. On his way back to the living room, a text came through from Will.

Who did dis bro? On God I'm killing whoever, he said.

Dontae hesitated to respond, but he was angry. So angry he wanted Omar to die.

Omar, he said.

Omar. Omar? Will texted back.

Yep.

Bet, Will said.

<u>24</u>

<u>Sharon</u>

Sharon walked through the front door of her home at approximately 9:50 pm. She'd just finished working ten hours at the Dollar General on Washington Avenue. Her coworker was a no-call-no-show, so she stayed past her five o'clock shift to help with coverage, and help close.

She took her black walking shoes off at the door — a rule she enforced in her home — and slouched on her living room couch. She was mentally and physically exhausted. Her brain hurt from dealing with rude costumers and the fast-paced job of a cashier, and her heels ached from standing on her feet for ten hours.

She was somewhat relieved after finally taking a seat, but she became irritable from the loud music blasting from William's bedroom. She tried her best to ignore it by grabbing a box of Kool's from her pocket, walking into kitchen, and lighting it on the gas stove with the butt of the cigarette in her mouth.

The bass mixed with cursing and William rapping along, however, couldn't be ignored. Sharon walked up to his bedroom door and started banging on it with her fist.

"Who is it?" he called.

"Boy, turn that mess down, I gotta headache," she yelled.

The volume went down and William opened the door. "Sorry, Ma, you take something for it?" he asked.

"No, William, it will go away if you stop blasting your music. Where is your brother?" she asked.

"He went to the gas station," William answered.

149

"Where ya'll going?" she asked.

"We bout to go up north."

"I told ya'll bout going up that highway. Them niggas in Chicago are crazy. I saw on the news 66 people shot and twelve dead," she said, taking a puff off the cigarette and blowing smoke out, her other hand on her hip.

"Ma we good, we not going around none of that," William said, laughing.

He was still standing in the doorway of his bedroom when his phone's text message alert went off. "That's Timmy, he outside," he said.

"Trust me, I know. I can hear the music," she said, her lips pursed. "Okay, baby, ya'll be safe out there. I love you. Tell your brother I love him, too."

"Love you too, Ma," he replied.

William walked towards the door. Sharon shook her head. "Can't tell these kids nothing," she muttered as she headed for the bathroom. She sat on the toilet and heard the front door shut.

A split second later, she jumped in terror after hearing multiple gunshots.

"William!" she screamed. She rose from the toilet quickly, grabbing toilet paper hysterically, wiping herself, and then pulling her slacks up as fast as she could.

She raced towards the front door, sliding on the slick tile in the kitchen. Sharon opened the door and stood on the porch, her heart racing and her mouth wide open. She cried silent tears and tried to scream, but nothing came out. Finally, she started panting and screamed out her youngest child's name.

She tried to run towards the car, but William grabbed her to hold her back. She fought through his hold, and he gave up and walked to the driver's side of the car. His stomach ached and his heart crumbled.

Sharon opened the passenger side door, climbed inside, and shook Timmy's lifeless body. "Timothy, baby," she cried. "No, no, no." She sobbed and held his blood-soaked body in her arms.

25

Jerome 2

Jerome woke up the next morning, and the first thing he did was check his phone for missed calls and text messages. He was pleased to see a message from Omar.

I've been thinking and you're right. I'm going back to school on Monday.

Eeee let's go, Jerome replied with a shocked face emoji to follow.

He rose from his bed as if Omar's revelation was the greatest news he'd heard all year. He slipped on a pair of white basketball shorts and black Nike slides and sat on the front porch, waiting on his mom to arrive

home from work. She was late coming home, but he

figured she stopped at Jewel to do some grocery

shopping, and maybe to the Shell on the corner of River

and Washington to pick up the newspaper before

coming home. It was always one or the other after work.

Her words and actions were so predictable they were

embedded in his brain.

He swiped down his Facebook timeline, and was

shocked to see several RIP Timmy posts. His heart

dropped. *I heard those gunshots*, he thought. He knew

that Tommy and Will lived on the next block over…and

he also knew that shortly after he heard the gunshots, he

saw Omar walking through his yard.

"Damn, O," he sighed. Jerome was smart enough

to put two and two together. And he had a gut feeling

that Omar was the shooter. He looked up at the house

across the street, and as much as he didn't want to

believe his friend was responsible, his actions were suspicious.

Moments later, his mom pulled up in her white 2018 Dodge Saturn, her slow jams blasting. She popped the trunk and he met her at the rear of the vehicle to help with the groceries.

"How was work?" he asked.

"It was work," she answered.

"You say that every day," he said, smiling.

"Well you ask me that every day knowing what I'm about to say," she said, smiling back.

She bent over slowly to sit on the steps, as if the night shift hours were exhausting. She read the front page of the paper while Jerome carried the four plastic bags of groceries upstairs to put them away. He put the groceries away frantically, anxious to get back outside to read the paper. He was convinced that Omar murdered Timmy, but he needed confirmation. He ran back down the stairs as soon as he finished, his heart racing, but not from the split second of cardio. The anticipation was killing him.

He sat down next to his mother, who read the paper with a frown upon her face. He read over her shoulder to see if there were any leads. It didn't take him long to gather information on the shooting.

"See, this is why we need to move. Did you hear any gunshots last night?" she asked.

"Yeah, they woke me up," he said.

"Sharon's son got killed last night," she said. "Lord have mercy, that poor woman. And I know his daddy is losing his mind. What's wrong with these kids? These gangs are getting outta hand."

Jerome dropped his head, contemplating whether or not he should mention Omar, but his mother brought him up instead.

Omar and his mom walked out of their house, both waving as they got in her white Jeep Cherokee. Jerome and his mom waved back.

"You need to stay away from that boy," she said.

"Why?"

"I see him down the street at that dope house on my way to work. You don't wanna ruin your scholarship. I know he's your friend, but you have to recognize when you outgrow people. Ya'll headed in opposite directions. Life is about choices. One bad decision can cost you everything. You're about to go to Harvard, and it's sad to say if he in these streets, he's gonna be dead or in jail."

Jerome sat quietly, soaking in his mother's words as he stared off into space.

"Do you understand me?" she asked.

Jerome nodded his head yes.

She asked again with authority. "Do you understand me?"

"Yes. Yes ma'am," he said, stuttering.

She handed him the paper, kissed him on the cheek, and told him she loved him. Jerome said it back while looking at the Daily Journal with the slain teenager's mugshot on the front page. The headline read "Local Basketball Star Gunned Down."

His mother rose to her feet, stretching her arms and yawning before opening the screen door. "I'm about to go to bed," she said while patting the side of her head to soothe an itch. "Make sure you take the trash out. The garbage truck will be through here in a few," she added.

Jerome rose to his feet and followed his mother, his face still buried in the paper. The article offered little to no information on the shooting. Timothy Sutton was shot multiple times while sitting in a vehicle outside his home on South Rosewood, and there were no suspects.

He was deeply saddened, yet disappointed that there were no leads. He watched The First 48 faithfully. He was headed to law school. He was obsessed with crime and catching the bad guys. He pulled the draw strings tight, and lifted the black trash bag out of the garbage can in the kitchen and carried it downstairs while simultaneously browsing through stories on Instagram. Several of his followers posted photos of Timothy in their feed. He dropped the bag on the side of the trash can, locked his phone, and put it in his back pocket. He lifted the top off the blue trash can and picked the bag up, to drop it in, but he dropped the bag on the pavement instead. His heart raced yet again, but this time his head and palms were sweating. He gazed inside the trashcan with his eye wide open and his eyebrows raised.

On the inside of the can, stuffed on the side of a box and under a bag, was the handle of a 9 millimeter handgun.

Jerome surveyed the area to see if anyone was watching, then reached inside the can, grabbed the gun out, and stuffed it in the front of his jeans.

Part 6

26

Kyla 2

Will agreed to watch the kids Saturday night at seven,

but he hated Kyla and he felt she was partly responsible

for his brother's death.

Kyla was insensitive towards his loss, calling him

repeatedly, but he ignored her phone calls. She walked

through the kitchen with the phone in one hand and her

six-month-old son, Malik, on her hip. Her head was

wrapped with a multicolored rag to hold her hairstyle in

place, and she had on pink boy shorts and a pink sports

bra from Victoria's Secret. Hunger pangs had Malik

screaming at the top of his lungs, tears pouring down his

cheeks and onto his chubby chest and potbelly. All he wore was a soaked diaper, and his hair was pulled back in a single puff-ball.

After setting her cell phone on the stove, she put three scoops of Similac and infant rice in a bottle filled with nursery water, put the top on it, and shook it vigorously. Her two-year-old daughter, Kari, was glued to her side, repeatedly saying, "Mommy. I'm hungry."

Kyla responded emphatically, "Kari, go sit yo ass down and watch TV like I told you!"

The little girl ran back into the living room, screaming, as Kyla handed Malik his bottle, finally silencing his cries. She picked up her phone and called Will again, but decided to leave a voice message this time.

"You know who it is, leave it," said Will on the voicemail greeting, followed by a beep.

"William, you said you was watching the kids tonight. I need a break! I'm bringing them there whether you answer the phone or not," she yelled.

She called him right back, but the voicemail picked up again. "Ughh," she growled, tears in her eyes. Kyla was eighteen years old, with two kids, and next to no help from their father. She had *had* it.

She poured Kari a bowl of Fruity Pebbles and sat her at the kitchen table, which gave her a few minutes of time to gather her thoughts. She retreated to her gray suede sofa, her heart filled with regret, wishing she could do it all over again. "I shoulda listened," she said, sighing.

Kyla's mother, Patricia, would always preach (as she called it) about not focusing on boys.

"Why do you want to grow up so fast? These boys don't care nothing about you. They're just out for one thing. You don't want to be tied down with children

164

at a young age. Finish school. Go to college. Your education is important."

Blah, blah, blah, was all Kyla thought at the time.

Patricia could tell when her words fell on deaf ears, so she would end her sermon by saying, "A hard head makes a soft ass. Don't say I didn't tell you."

And still Kyla didn't care. She'd just roll her eyes and say, "Okay, Ma, I heard you."

Patricia only met Will once and warned Kyla about the bad vibes she'd gotten in his presence. He visited one evening, claiming Kyla was tutoring him in algebra. He didn't take his Timberland boots off at the door, which was a pet peeve of hers.

"Young man, please take your shoes off at the door," she admonished. She took one look at his French braids, endless tattoos, and sagging skinny-jeans, and Kyla knew she wasn't impressed. And when he spoke, he didn't look her ma in the eye.

"I hope you don't call yourself liking this boy. He's gonna use you up and leave you with a broken heart," she said.

"Momma he's not like that," said Kyla, sighing.

Kyla took her mother's warnings as hate because she was infatuated with Will, and she'd do anything to make him happy...even if it meant disobeying her mom's rules and giving up her innocence by losing her virginity.

Will asked Kyla to send him naked photos via text after school that day. She'd never sent pictures like that before, but she was obsessed with him, and she loved the attention. She did her makeup, straightened her shoulder length hair, glued fake eyelashes on, put red lipstick on her full lips, and stood in front of the full-length mirror on the back of her bedroom door. She took several nudes, exposing every inch of her chocolate skin, her face included. He sent her pictures too, but only of his private parts.

Then the nudes prompted him to ask her about sex. She knew it was coming, and she was afraid, but she could already feel the pressure.

You scared or something? He messaged, sending her the smirking face emoji.

She searched for a response that would impress him. *I'm not scared. I've been waiting on you.*

They spoke at length that evening and made plans for a future encounter. They ended the text thread with Will saying *I love you*. She smiled from ear to ear. He never said he loved her out loud, but it was enough to lure her in and get what he wanted. Will was one of the most popular guys at Kankakee High. He was Homecoming King at the last winter ball, he was cute, he had a car, he sold drugs, and he was in one of the most popular gangs in the city.

She talked the talk that night, but when the weekend came, it was time to walk the walk.

Her ma was exhausted that night after working the day shift, so she was sound asleep by ten. Deep down inside, Kyla was hoping Will wouldn't mention sex, but when the clock struck 10:05 pm, he texted, *you ready?* With the thinking face emoji.

I can't come out this late, I'll get in trouble, Kyla typed, quickly ending it with the sad-faced emoji.

Wait till she go to sleep and sneak out, Will replied. *I'll come pick you up*, he offered.

She was out of excuses. She felt pressured to back up everything she said while sexting him, so she took his advice. With her mom in bed, she climbed out her bedroom window and met Will, who had parked at the corner in his Caprice. Will drove to Bird's Park, parked his car under the bridge, and they had sex on the backseat. It was her first time, but he had plenty of experience.

The experience for her, however, wasn't enjoyable at all. She was in so much pain that she bled and cried the whole time. Afterwards, Will dropped her off at the corner and she climbed back into her bedroom through the window.

Kyla was so disgusted with herself after having sex with Will that night that she showered and scrubbed her body vigorously. She sent Will several texts, but he did not answer. The following day at school, many of the boys in her classes were staring at her, sniggling and giggling, but she did not know why.

Her friend Tierra had to tell her. "Girl, why you send that nigga those nudes? He posted them on Facebook."

Kyla went on Facebook and saw the post. "Kankakee hoes Exposed." Her heart shattered into a thousand pieces. She confronted Will at his locker in between classes, and his response was cold-blooded.

"I thought you loved me," she cried.

"We don't love these hoes," he laughed.

His friends laughed, too. She couldn't take the pain, the embarrassment, and the shame it caused. She walked out of school that day, vowing to never return. Kyla was a straight-A student when she dropped out of school as a sophomore, and a month after she lost her virginity, she found out she was pregnant with Kari. She hid the pregnancy from her mother for as long as she could.

27

Riley & Chloe

Chloe called Riley on her break that evening, with guilt weighing heavy on her heart. She'd finally realized how stupid it was to attack Kelly, but she didn't know how to apologize.

"I'm sure she hates my guts," Chloe said.

"Yeah, you're a twat waffle so she probably does...but what happened? Why the change of heart?" Riley asked.

"I'm just tired of everyone talking about it. There's not a day goes by that someone isn't mentioning the fight to me so I can imagine how she feels. Plus, after thinking about it...she was right. Jason chose her."

"Aww, my BFF is growing up," Riley said. "Is Jason at work tonight?"

"No, he hasn't been here in weeks. I think he quit. Should I give her a call?" Chloe asked.

"I say go for it. What's the worst she can say?"

"Um, go to hell you dumb bitch. Stop calling me you twat-waffle," laughed Chloe. "I feel horrible and I want to make it right."

"I have an idea. Ask her if she wants to go to Jerome's party with us. We can all hang out," Riley said excitedly.

"Okay, I'll try. She'll probably just ignore my calls."

Chloe took Riley's advice and called Kelly before her break was over. She sat at one of the booths with a large raspberry tea and a medium curly fry, her phone to her ear, nervously anticipating her ex-friend's answer. Kelly didn't pick up, so she sighed with disappointment. She called again, but Kelly didn't answer so she left a voice message.

"Hey, Kels. I know you have every reason to hate me, because if I was you I'd hate me, too. I'm calling to apologize for attacking you. Like, it was really stupid. I hope you'll find it in your heart to forgive me."

Chloe paused, searching for the words, and her voice wavered as her eyes began to tear up. "I'm going to Riley's boyfriend's party tonight and I thought it would be cool if we all went together. Just like old times. But shoot me a text or something; let me know how you feel. If not, I totally understand. Again, I'm sorry."

28

Jason & Kelly

Jason couldn't sleep because of the withdrawal symptoms. He was sweating profusely and itching like he had hives. He didn't have a dime to his name to satisfy his addiction, and after hours of contemplating solutions that wouldn't get him jail time, he decided to sell his Xbox 360 and all the games with it.

He texted Kelly and asked her for a ride at six am, but she didn't write back. He walked to one of his former classmate's house in the pouring rain and sold the game system to him for a hundred dollars...much less than what it was worth.

Kelly texted him back as he walked down Broadway. *Hey, what's up?* He didn't want to shoot up at his parents' house just in case he overdosed. He'd shot up in front of Kelly plenty of times, and wanted to do it in her car. The anxiousness was replaced with joy when he saw her response.

I got some if you want to try it now, he wrote.

I don't know, Jason, I'm scared.

Don't be. We will do it together, he wrote.

Be there in 2 minutes, wait by the Legion, she said.

Kelly was still in love with the jock and star quarterback of the Bradley Bourbonnais football team, who was so popular that he couldn't go anywhere in town without someone acknowledging him. What Jason had become was a far cry from the kid who had a promising future, however. He'd become an addict, who saw everyone and everything around him as a means to an end.

Kelly was afraid, but the world around her had crumbled, and she was still dealing with the aftermath of being bullied by her peers. Weeks after Chloe attacked her she was suffering from depression, searching for an out, but every turn she made was a dead end.

Then an incoming call on her cell phone arrived that shocked her as if she'd seen a ghost. "Chloe" lit up on her screen, which made her heart rate increase rapidly. *Why won't she just leave me alone?*

Kelly's eyes began to tear as she declined the call and kept driving. She parked the car at a shopping center and her adrenaline began to pump.

"I can't do it," she said, chickening out now that the opportunity was there.

"Come on, Kels. You love me, don't you? We're just having fun," he pleaded.

She loved him dearly, and she'd do anything to make him happy. He loved her, too. He didn't view the drug as a bad thing. He thought he was doing her a favor by exposing her to the drug. He said it helped him forget about how painful the world was and he wanted her to be pain free.

"Try it once and I'll never ask you again," he insisted.

She looked him in his eyes, and she began to utter no, but her cell phone rang. Once again it was Chloe. She frowned while looking at the screen, easing her thumb towards accepting the call, but once again she declined. *Why is she still bothering me.*

Fuck it.

"Okay, Jason, if it will make you happy. I'll try it once," she said, sighing. "Just once."

Jason tied a black cord around her skinny arm tightly, and smacked her arm repeatedly until several blue veins appeared. Her chest rose quickly in fear as Jason brought the needle closer to her arm.

"You have to calm down. Take a deep breath," he advised in a soothing voice.

"Okay," she said, inhaling deeply.

"Are you ready?" he asked.

"Will you just do it?" she asked tightly.

He stuck the needle in her arm, and her chest rose and came down slowly. She was extremely drowsy almost immediately, and her head started nodding. She became slightly incoherent.

"How do you feel?" he asked.

She could hear him, but his voice sounded muffled. She tried to speak, but her speech was slurred.

"How do you feel?" he asked again.

Seconds later, Kelly started having spasms, jerking and seizing.

And then foaming at the mouth.

"Kelly!" he screamed, reaching out to grab her. He looked at her in terror as the seizing stopped and her skin grew pale. Kelly gasped for air, and Jason looked around the parking lot, unsure of what to do. He pulled his phone out to dial 911, but he realized he could go to jail if the cops came. He bit his fingernails and pounded his fist on the dashboard, filled with regret.

Kelly's phone rang again and he grabbed it, peering at the screen. It was a voice message from Chloe. "Kels?" He yelled, shaking her in an attempt to revive her. In the moment of anxiousness, only one thing could calm him.

He grabbed the spoon from the cup holder, put fire to it with a red lighter, and filled the same needle with heroin. He tied a cord around his arm, put the needle in his vein, and nodded out.

29

Riley

Riley was conflicted. Her boyfriend of nearly five months invited her to a party to celebrate the biggest achievement of his young life, but her parents would *kill* her if they knew she was in Kankakee. It was forbidden territory in their eyes, but she loved Jerome and didn't want to disappoint him. She sat on her black and white polka dot stool and did her makeup, while staring beyond her reflection in the Linon Biltmore vanity mirror.

She placed the mini Chanel gold hoop earrings her father bought her in her ears, which reminded her of the bitterness she felt towards him. She reflected on a heated discussion she had at the dinner table with her parents a few months before.

"We're not racist, love-bug. We're just saying everyone should be with their own kind," her father said. Riley looked somberly at her own reflection as she recalled sitting at the dinner table, twirling her pasta with her fork, staring angrily down at her plate. *I finally meet a guy who loves me and my parents hate him,* she thought. At sixteen years old, Riley was overweight, but highly developed for her age. Most of the white guys at BBCHS made fun of her by calling her fat, or they totally ignored her.

"What am I supposed to do? The guys at my school are into skinny girls," she replied, rolling her eyes.

"That's not true. Brice has the hots for her," her brother Ted said.

"The hots is right. Brice just wants to get in my pants," Riley argued.

"We can get you a membership at Fitness Premiere," Mom said. "I hear they have a nice boot-camp class there."

"Great, Mom, so you agree I'm a lard ass," Riley screeched.

"Brice is a good kid and he comes from a good family," her father assured her.

"You mean Brice is white?" Riley challenged.

Her father sighed deeply. He was quick-tempered, but he maintained his composure. "Bottom line is...you can't talk to this Jesse, Jamal or whatever the hell his name is, and we don't want you hanging out in Kankakee with those thugs. You have no idea what I see on the job in that city," he stressed.

"His name is Jerome and he's not like that," Riley bit back. "He's smart. He applied to Harvard!"

"Riley Marie Shaffer, you do not use that tone with your father, young lady," yelled her mother.

Riley pushed back her chair from the table. "I'm done."

Her mother sighed. "Finish your food first."

"I lost my appetite," Riley said, folding her arms and pouting.

"I'm sure he's a good kid," her dad said, "but he's not for you."

Riley stomped up the stairs, slammed her bedroom door, buried her face in her pillow, and cried herself to sleep. She was deeply saddened by her parent's disapproval, but determined to keep talking to Jerome.

The discussion over dinner took place a few days after a basketball game at Kankakee High School. Ted was the starting forward for the BBCHS basketball team, and Riley attended the game along with her parents.

There was snow on the ground, and the roads were slick from slush and black ice. Riley was dressed in blue jeans, black half high Columbia boots, a red BBCHS sweater and coat, a red plaid scarf, and earmuffs. She sat in the upper bleachers with her parents on the opposite side of the opposing team, cheering for the Boilermakers. The small gym was packed with fans, who were all excited to attend the cross-town rivalry.

At halftime, Riley asked her dad for cash to go to the concession stand, and he agreed. "As long as you bring me a Pepsi, and your mom a bag of Chili-Fritos," he laughed.

Riley clutched the cash in her palm, took the stairs down to the first floor, and went out the side doors to the lunch room where the snacks and refreshments were being sold. She stood in line, contemplating what she'd buy with the twenty bucks her father gave her, when Jerome walked up wearing a camouflage hooded coat, white tee-shirt, blue jeans, and tan Timberland boots. He brushed the top of his tapered fade and stood in line directly behind her.

He watched as Riley bought a bag of Fritos, two Pepsi's, M&M's, and a bag of popcorn. After gathering the change from the student worker, Riley realized she couldn't carry all of the snacks alone.

"You need some help?" asked Jerome.

She smiled but said, "No, thank you. I can make two trips."

"And miss this game? Halftime is almost over," he smiled.

"I guess you're right." She grinned. "If you don't mind."

The two teens walked back to where Riley's parents sat. Riley felt extremely nervous, and Jerome contemplated how he could get her phone number. She handed her dad the Pepsi, Mom the Frito's, and Jerome handed her the popcorn and the other Pepsi. Mom and Dad both had inquisitive looks upon their faces, wondering who he was.

"Mom, Dad this is…sorry I never asked you your name," she laughed, red-faced.

"Jerome," he said with a smile.

"Jerome was nice enough to help me carry the snacks," Riley said.

Both Mom and Dad smiled, but they offered no words. Their unwillingness to speak made Jerome feel awkward, but he was still respectful.

"Nice to meet you," he said. "Hey listen, do you want to come down to watch the game?" he asked her.

Riley was taken back by the request, but said, "Sure, why not?"

She left with Jerome, but her parents were clearly not happy. Riley, on the other hand, enjoyed herself. They talked the entire time and paid very little attention to the second half of the competitive basketball game. Jerome shared details of his life. He lived in Kankakee on Greenwood with his mother, who worked nights at Shapiro Developmental Center. He applied to many colleges, but hoped to go to Harvard Law School. Riley told him that her mom was an RN at Riverside Hospital, and her dad was a detective for the city of Kankakee. She applied to colleges close to home, but hoped to go to U of I. They exchanged numbers.

Four and a half months later, she was invited to a party to celebrate his full ride to Harvard.

After reflecting on her parent's unwillingness to accept Jerome, she became agitated. She refused to adopt their views. Jerome was a loving person, who was smart and had a bright future. He had no hidden agendas, and

187

she appreciated the fact that he wasn't pressuring her to have sex. She decided to go against their wishes. She wasn't going to disappoint Jerome for a hateful reason like the color of his skin or the neighborhood he lived in.

Riley left home at approximately 9:30, dressed in a baby blue Kankakee Kays sweater Jerome had given her, a pair of dark blue jeans, and white Air-Max Nikes. She drove to Chloe's house, pulling into the driveway, and honked the horn. She sent a text. *Chloe I'm outside, come on. Did you hear back from Kelly? I hope she's going with.*

Chloe didn't reply, and she didn't read the message. Riley wasn't worried, but she thought it was weird that Chloe wasn't responding. She always replied quickly because she always had her phone in her hand.

Riley looked at the house and it was dark, as if no one was home. She waited five minutes for the rain to ease up, and then got out to knock on the door and ring the doorbell. No one answered. She went back to the car, frustrated with her friend. *You suck. I guess I'm going alone,* she texted.

Riley backed out of the driveway. Her phone rang, which calmed her spirits. She expected to see "BFF" on her screen for Chloe, but it said "Mom."

30

Lynn

Lynn stopped her car at a red light at the intersection of Entrance and Court Street. There was a slight drizzle of rain dropping on the windshield, but not enough to turn the wipers on. Elton John's "Tiny Dancer" played at a low volume on the stereo, and she sang along while staring at the light, anticipating the moment it would turn green.

She was dressed in light blue scrubs and white cross trainers, the normal attire for her graveyard shift in the ER at Riverside Hospital. For some odd reason she felt compelled to call Riley, who had been in her bedroom when Lynn left for work. She put her cell phone on the Bluetooth loud speaker in the car, and went to her recent calls where she found Riley's name at the top. She made a left onto Court Street, waiting on Riley to pick up. When she did, she could tell that her daughter wasn't home.

"Hey sweetie, I didn't know you were leaving," she said. "Where are you going?"

"Mom," Riley sighed.

Lynn paused. "You're going to the party, aren't you?"

There was a moment of silence, outside of the breeze on Riley's end. Her car windows must be cracked and wind was blowing.

"I tried to get Chloe to go with me, but I guess she's busy," Riley said.

"It's okay," Lynn, replied. "I understand; you don't have to explain. Just know that your father means well. He doesn't want anything bad to happen to you."

"Jerome is not like that, and I know plenty of white guys who wish they could get into Harvard. I'm not gonna stay long, I promise," Riley insisted.

Lynn sighed while shaking her head and grinding her teeth to ease the tension. She was conflicted. She was raised during a time when interracial dating was forbidden, and now her precious daughter was head-over-heels for someone black. She also felt bad for going against her husband's wishes, but she wanted Riley to be happy. She wanted her to have the same memories that she had with her first love...even if it was with someone of a different race.

"Be careful." Lynn's voice wobbled and tears blurred her vision, then fell down her cheeks. "Tell Jermaine I said hi."

"Mom, his name is *Jerome*, but I'll tell him. I love you," Riley, said, giggling.

"Sorry sweetie," Lynn laughed. "I love you, too."

Lynn ended the call, feeling somewhat relieved. She admired her daughter's will to love, and she felt closer to her after the conversation. She parked her car in the hospital garage, lowered the visor, and opened the mirror to see how bad her makeup had smeared. Her face was stained with streaks black eye-liner. "Great," she said, taking a deep breath.

31

Jerome 3

Jerome's conscience was eating at him and the guilt of inviting Omar made him feel worse. He could hear Ma's voice in the back of his mind. *You have to recognize when you outgrow people.* If she knew he was throwing a juke party in her house, she'd beat the living daylights out of him, but to him it was worth the risk.

Because on top of his secret gathering, he had a murder weapon hidden in his bedroom.

After finding the 9 mm Omar hid in their trash can, he brought it into the house and stashed it at the top of his closet. He intended to talk to Omar about the gun privately when he arrived at the party. He didn't know what the outcome would be, but he was trying to be a good friend. Wouldn't his mom approve of that?

By nine pm, he was dressed and anxiously awaiting Riley's arrival. Around 10:15 pm, Riley sent him a text. He already had his phone in his hand, so he read it immediately.

Chloe stood me up but I'm omw. Did you tell mom yet?

He still hadn't told his ma that he was dating a white girl, but after reading Riley's text, he sent Ma a message saying, *I got something to tell you.*

Velma replied immediately. *What you gotta tell me?*

It's about my girlfriend.

Rhonda?

No Ma, it's Riley, he typed.

Excuse me LOL, what about Riley? She asked.

LOL she's different, he texted, smirking.

Ok different how?

...She's a white girl? LOL, he typed, his heart racing.

Velma took a moment to respond, which had Jerome on the edge of his seat. He knew she would feel some type of way, because she believed that everyone should date their own kind. Maybe, just this once, she could put her feelings to the side.

Ok when do I get to meet her? She asked.

For real? Relief washed over Jerome.

What you mean for real? You think your snow bunny too good to meet me?

No I just thought you would trip because she's white, he wrote.

"*Baby as long as she loves you, I love her,* his ma said.

How about tomorrow? He asked.

If that works for you, she replied.

Jerome responded to Riley's text as if the discussion had already taken place. *Of course. She wants to meet you tomorrow.*

Riley replied with hearts and smiley face emoji's. *I'll see you soon,* she texted.

Riley called Chloe several times on her way to the party for an explanation, but she did not answer. "I should have known," she mumbled, frustrated. She sent Jerome several texts on her way to his house, once avoiding an accident after taking her eyes off of the road.

She pulled up in front of his house in her red Passat with a card and a gift for Jerome. The house was packed with teens when she arrived...and some of them wore RIP Timmy t-shirts with his face on the front.

Jerome opened the door with a smile on his face that was contagious enough to make Riley smile, too. They hugged and kissed, and she handed him his gift.

"What's this for?" he asked, backing up for her to enter.

"Umm, you're going to *Harvard*. That's kind of a big deal," Riley gushed, stepping inside.

"Thanks," Jerome said with a twinkle in his eye.

"Wow. I didn't expect this many people here." She had to yell over the music as she looked around the packed room.

She was amazed at the sight of teens juking, which was something she'd never experienced. They walked through the crowded living room and dining room and into the kitchen, where snacks were set up on table.

"My homeboy Omar supposed to bring some alcohol," Jerome said. "He should be here any minute now." He checked his blue-faced watch with the brown leather band.

"I don't really drink," Riley said. "But...maybe a beer," she relented.

"You're beautiful," Jerome said, grabbing her by the hand and kissing her again.

"You look nice, too," Riley said, smiling again to hide her shyness. She looked him up and down, surveying his stone washed black jeans, black and red Jordan 4's, and a white t-shirt with Timmy's face on it.

"Is that the dude who got shot?" Riley asked. "I saw the posts online."

Jerome shook his head yes.

"I'm sorry. Were you close?" she asked.

"Not really, but I knew him. Everyone decided to wear the shirts for the night," said Jerome.

There was a brief silence, and Jerome grabbed Styrofoam cups and began to pour soda.

"I can't believe your mom wants to meet me," Riley said.

"I know, right? I was bugging. I thought she was gonna trip on you being white," he said.

"She's a lot more accepting than my parents," Riley replied.

Their discussion was cut short when Jerome's phone ranged. He grabbed it from his pocket and saw that Omar texted him.

Come open the door.

Ok, Jerome replied.

Jerome walked to the door and Riley followed. It seemed like the walk of a lifetime. Jerome was bobbing his head to the music, shaking hands with a few of his buddies from school. Riley was smiling and waving back at those who greeted her. The night was young.

"Oh my," Riley exclaimed, her eyes widening after seeing a girl back her derrière up on a boy. Jerome laughed and looked back at Riley, who also laughed, just before opening the door.

Omar stood on the porch with two brown bags filled with bottles of Ciroc he'd gotten from Perry.

Jerome went to greet him, but his eyes widened after looking over Omar's shoulders and seeing two armed black males standing in the street.

"Get down," he screamed, just before falling to the floor. Omar slammed the door, ducked, and grabbed a gun from his waist in the process. Jerome reached out for Riley to pull her to the floor, but she ran in the other direction. He watched as she fell to the ground after a bullet shattered the living room window and hit her in the upper back.

Jerome jumped to his feet to run over to her, but he was also struck by the gunfire. There were many cries and screams being drowned out by the music as the bullets continued to riddle the home, hitting several other teens.

When the gunfire ceased, there was blood and bodies everywhere. Those who survived unharmed ran out the back door. Those who were harmed cried out in the silent aftermath.

32

<u>Dontae 4</u>

Dontae was still in a complete state of shock. He cried off and on for hours after Timmy's death, contemplating whether or not he should tell his mom that Omar was the shooter. Gloria was in constant communication with him, even more than usual.

Earlier that day she reminded him, "I know you're hurting baby, but you can talk to me about anything."

Nevertheless, he decided not to confide in her. Instead he chose to speak to Will, who was even more grief stricken. He called him from his bedroom, lying on his beck in his twin bed, staring at the ceiling with tears in his eyes. The pain in his heart was due partly to losing his friend but also to the fear of dying himself. He listened as Will spewed his plans to retaliate, and in that moment he realized what his mom had been saying all along.

"He can't hide forever," Will raged. "We gone drive by his momma crib and air that mother fucker out."

"Damn, you bout to shoot the whole house up? His mom might be in there," Dontae said.

"I don't give a fuck who in there, he killed my lil bro," Will said, sobbing. "We need to get that nigga tonight."

Dontae knew Will saying "we" meant that he wanted him to get involved. He was afraid to participate, but afraid to say no to a friend who was desperate, blind, and in need of someone to travel down the dark path with him so he wouldn't feel alone.

Dontae searched for a way to respond, but he couldn't.

"I know you rollin with us, ain't you?" asked Will. "Corey said he with the shit."

"I ain't never shot a gun before. Plus Mom's been watching me like a hawk," Dontae said, frowning.

"You know what, it's cool. You a lame, I knew you wasn't bout that life anyway," Will said, ending the call.

When Will hung up, Dontae felt a sense of relief. He looked out his bedroom window and watched as Will walked out the door five minutes after hanging up on him. He decided to make one more call to free himself of all the negativity.

Dontae called Tierra, expecting her not to answer. She'd been distant towards him since they skipped school that afternoon, but he had to get something off his chest. He was shocked when she answered the phone.

"Hey, boo. What you doing?" Tierra asked.

"Nothing much, just cooling," Dontae said.

"I'm getting ready to go to Jerome's party," she said. "You going?"

"Nah, I been on lock since Timmy got killed. Moms ain't letting me breath," Dontae replied. "But look, I know what your mom was talking about that day."

"What you mean?" Tierra asked.

"When she asked if you been taking your medicine," he stated.

"I told you she was talking about my birth control," Tierra lied.

"C'mon, bruh keep it one-hunnid. You gave me a STD," he cried.

Tierra was silent on the phone, and so was Dontae, waiting on the apology he felt he deserved.

"I'm sorry, my mom took me to the doctor and I thought it was gone," she cried. "I promise I didn't do it on purpose, Dontae."

Dontae hesitated, unsure of what to ask next. A part of him believed her, although he was still angry.

"Who gave it to you?" he asked.

"I don't know, but I think it was Corey," she said.

"Corey. Corey!" Dontae shouted.

"Yep, he burnt me."

After speaking to Tierra, Dontae was content with how his night went. He walked downstairs and sat next to his mom on the living room sofa, where she was watching television. He kissed her on the cheek and rested his head on her shoulder.

"Thanks, Ma," he said.

"For what?" she asked.

"For everything."

33

Will

Kyla did exactly what she said she would do. At approximately seven pm, she knocked on Will's front door with Kari standing next to her, holding her hand, and Malik's car seat on her arm. Sharon answered the door, happy to see her grandchildren.

"I'm sorry about your loss," Kyla said automatically. "Is William home? He said he would watch them tonight."

"Yes, he's here. William!" Sharon yelled.

William heard his mom calling him and walked out of his bedroom, shaking his head. "Hold up

Momma, I'm not watching them," Will protested. "I got something to do. Ask that nigga Perry to watch them."

"Shut up, boy; this is not your house, and my grandbabies can come over here anytime they want to," she argued.

"You can watch them then," he said, shaking his head again, then stalked back to his bedroom.

"Wow. I just can't with him," Kyla said, her eyebrows raised.

"Don't worry about it, baby. He taking the loss pretty hard," Sharon said.

"I understand. I need a break though. They with me twenty-four-seven," Kyla replied. "Don't tell him, but I'm going to a party," she added, smirking.

"Well good for you. I don't blame you. You need to have some fun sometimes. William doesn't understand the struggles of a single mom; he has a lot of growing up to do," his mother said.

Kyla left, anxious to have some free time, and Sharon spent time with her grandchildren in the living room.

Upstairs, Will sat on the edge of his bed, talking on his phone with Corey.

"I just talked to Dontae. That nigga scared to ride. Talking bout he never shot a gun before and how mommy got him on lock," Will said.

"But when he wanted to go to Tierra party, he was willing to risk it all," Corey said. "It's for the best anyway. That nigga would probably snitch if we get bumped."

"I think we should get Omar tonight. You still getting Granny's car? Five-O still got my shit. We can drive by the crib, air that bitch out and dip," said Will.

"Yeah she knocked out, I already got the keys, but you know he stay across the street from Jerome, right?"

"And?" Will asked.

"His party tonight, it's probably gonna be a gang of mother fuckas outside," Corey replied.

"Right, well we gonna strap up and just roll through there. If we don't see nobody outside, we'll shoot the crib up. If we do we'll keep going and we'll catch em another day," Will said.

"Okay. I'll load the choppers and take em outside now," Corey said.

He walked out of his bedroom and down the stairs. His expression cast more fears on his mother, who was already grief stricken.

Sharon was terrified after Will told her he was leaving for a while. There was an agonizing sense of foreboding, eating the mature diva alive on the inside. She had no knowledge of his conversation, but she had a gut feeling he was going to retaliate based on that look on his face. Her heart was heavy and her throat ached as her grandchildren bawled at the sight of their father preparing to leave.

"William, you need to stay in the house with your children. Can't you see that they miss you? You never spend time with them," she said, hoping his children's cries would sway him to stay.

"Momma, I'm not going to be gone long," he said, pulling his red hoodie over his head, ignoring her pleas.

"You're about to go do something stupid; I can feel it. I already lost one son. I don't want to lose the only one I got left," she pleaded.

"I'm just going to kick it with the guys. I'm trying to get my mind off stuff," he said, lying through the gap in his front teeth.

"Can't they come over here?" she suggested.

"Momma, I'll be back," he said, looking her in the eyes.

"Lord have mercy, William. You never listen, but all I can do is pray for you," she said.

Will walked out the door, leaving his ma to tend to his children, with blood in his eyes and murder on his mind.

He walked down the street to Corey's house, scrolling through his phone, looking at pictures of Timmy while listening to the last song they recorded together with his ear buds in his ears. The sound of Timmy's voice and the sight of his face saddened him, but his anger towards Omar would not let him cry.

He texted Corey, *I'm out back*, and stood at the backdoor of his grandma's four bedroom home, waiting on Corey to open up. Corey opened the door, also wearing a hoodie, then they went to the garage where his granny's white 1985 Ford Ltd was parked.

Corey twisted the handle on the outside of the garage, lifted it up, then opened the trunk. Both teens grabbed an AK-47. Corey got in on the driver's side, and Will on the passenger side. There was more anger and rage in Will's heart than nervousness or panic. He knew who killed his brother, and he wanted him to pay for it.

They drove slowly down Greenwood, heading north towards Omar's crib. Corey looked left at the home, preparing to stop, but there was a surprise revelation.

Will spotted Omar just as he crossed the street with two brown bags in hand. He headed for Jerome's porch, looking down at his phone, dressed in a polo shirt, blue jeans, and black Jordan 5's…and totally unaware he was a moving target.

"There go that bitch ass nigga. Stop the car," Will said.

Corey put the car in park, stopping in the middle of the street directly in front of Jerome's house. They covered their faces with black ski-masks, and the two teens hopped out of the car, leaving both doors open, and both weapons in hand.

They aimed their rifles in Omar's direction and fired multiple rounds as he stood in the suddenly open doorway. Bullets scattered everywhere: the front door and windows, splitting the wooden porch support slats, piercing the siding, whizzing through the curtains, and shattering the glass.

"Die, motherfucker. You killed my brother!" screamed Will.

Suddenly, the shots started coming from another direction, causing Corey to retreat back to their get-away-car.

"Come on man, let's go," yelled Corey, slamming the driver's door and lifting his mask. He watched as Will continued shooting, totally disregarding the return fire.

Finally Will raced to the car and slammed the passenger door shut, but the shots kept coming in their direction. Both ducked their heads as Corey smashed on the gas, but the car veered to the left after a single bullet shattered the rear window.

And hit Corey in the back of his head.

The bullet killed him instantly. His head lolled as blood poured from the wound, but his foot still rested on the gas pedal. The car sped through the intersection and onto Station Street.

Will tried to intervene by grabbing the steering wheel, but a yellow H2 Hummer slammed into the rear passenger door. The airbags popped out of the Hummer and rendered the female driver unconscious.

Will tried to open the passenger door, but it was jammed. He panicked after hearing sirens in the background of the H2 Hummer's stuck horn, and then he climbed over the backseat and opened the rear driver's door. He exited the vehicle and tried to run, but

before he could take off he heard:

"If you move, I'll blow your fucking head off."

34

Sharon 2

Sharon had reached her maximum tolerance of pain. She couldn't grieve Timmy's death while she feared what William would do at the same time. Her heart couldn't take it. When he walked out the door, she knew she'd get a call saying he was either dead or in jail. Not only did she feel like a prisoner in her own home, but she felt like the world was tormenting her, as if shackles were on her brain and she couldn't break free from the painful memories.

She sat on the living room floor to play with her grandkids, then fed them dinner. Kyla picked them up early, saying she changed her mind about the party. Afterwards, Sharon went to the kitchen and grabbed a water bottle from the refrigerator.

Normally she'd pray, but she'd lost all faith. She turned the lamp on, set her water bottle on the night stand, and went to the bathroom. Sharon sat on the toilet for a few minutes, breathing rapidly, and pulled at the sides of her hair as thoughts of Timmy's body slumped in the car replayed vividly in her mind.

She washed her hands and looked up in the mirror with a blank stare, searching for a reason to keep fighting. A single tear drop rolled down her cheek, and she blinked excessively while reaching the same conclusion she had earlier. Sharon opened the medicine cabinet, grabbed a bottle of Ambien, and sat on the edge of her bed as she twisted the white bottle cap off.

Lord forgive me, she thought. She poured the entire bottle in the palm of her hand, dumped them in her mouth, and chugged down half of the water bottle. After drying her eyes, she turned the lamp off, hid under the covers, and closed her eyes.

Part 7

35

Detectives Shaffer and Moore

Detectives Shaffer and Moore sat in a black unmarked vehicle outside of a residence on South Greenwood. The home had been flagged as housing a possible suspect in the murder of Timothy Sutton.

Perry was the primary suspect, but as they had no concrete evidence, he was only wanted for questioning. They believed he murdered Timmy in retaliation for the beat down he suffered at the Amoco gas station a few weeks prior.

Shaffer was the more seasoned detective at 51 years old. He was a tall, muscular man with brown hair shorn down to a military buzz cut. Detect Moore was a 35-year-old African-American male; an Iraq vet and a newly-promoted detective. Shaffer was six months from retiring. He was a very talkative individual, who could carry on for his entire shift telling stories about his life experiences in an attempt to provide wisdom to the more youthful officers.

Shaffer took a sip of coffee, placed the mug in the holder, and began lecturing Moore about how stupid racism was. Moore hardly paid attention when Shaffer went on his rants, so he sat quietly in the passenger seat and continued eating his glazed donut and drinking coffee from a blue Chicago Bears cup.

"Ya wanna know why I moved from the South?" Shaffer asked, his southern accent pronounced. "I moved because the hate was so strong it caused some to disregard the most important things in life. I was born and raised in Little Rock, Arkansas, during the Jim Crow era. My old man owned a convenience store. I remember him being pissed when Eisenhower sent the troops to escort the Little Rock 9 into Central High. I was about 10 years old maybe. My sister was a sophomore in high school and he did not want her around "coloreds." The violence was out of control.

"Something had to be done," he said while throwing his hands up. "They were spitting on these kids and calling them coons and everything else but the children of God. One of the girls had acid thrown in her eyes; one was pushed down a flight of stairs. It was crazy. The colored schools didn't have the same resources as our schools, but in sixty-three, everything changed. The signs came down because everything was separate, and I mean *everything*: water fountains, restrooms, even swimming pools. There were restrooms with arrows pointing in opposite directions, whites and colored. Of course many businesses started accepting coloreds' but with a bit of reluctance. They'd sell them food but they couldn't dine in. Some would only take orders in the back of the building, in the alleyway, as if they were animals. Some had signs that read, *We serve colored but carry out only*. My dad still kept his sign up: *No Niggers Allowed*."

Moore was about to take another sip from his coffee cup, but he paused. He cut his eyes at Shaffer, looking him upside his head like he'd lost his damn mind. Veins were popping out his forehead, and he scowled after Shaffer's use of the word nigger.

The talkative detective was immediately apologetic. "No disrespect intended, but there's a point to my story," he said. "Anyway, he'd tell me with a sense of pride that a white man has no business taking nigger money. I didn't understand it, ya know? I mean, green is green no matter who hands it to you. At the end of the day the color of money is still green, and I loved it enough, even as a kid to not let something as stupid as the color of someone's skin to come between me and my money. That old saying is true: "Money talks and bullshit walks." My father's store ended up going out of business because he allowed his foolish pride to get in the way. He couldn't compete. The other crackers were smart because they didn't allow their racist views to impact their business. We struggled after the store closed," Shaffer rambled on, shaking his head.

Suddenly a call came through from dispatch. "Officers needed at a shooting in the 400 block of Greenwood," the dispatcher said. "A 1985 Ford Ltd was involved, and we believe this same vehicle is also involved in a car accident at the intersection of Station and Greenwood, with a yellow H2 Hummer."

"Damn it, that's right up the block," Moore swore.

"So much for a peaceful night," Shaffer grouched while smashing on the gas.

They hit the lights, turned on the sirens, and drove North on Greenwood, startled by the sounds of screams, and several kids running in the opposite direction. They stopped at the intersection of Station and Greenwood, exiting their vehicle cautiously, their weapons drawn as they slowly approached the Ford Ltd. The driver's side of the vehicle was occupied, but someone else was moving on the passenger side the vehicle. Both officers braced themselves, holding their handguns tightly.

The rear driver's side door swung open, and a black male hopped out frantically.

"Put your hands where I can see them!" yelled Moore.

"Put your hands up. If you move, I'll blow your fucking head off," yelled Shaffer.

"Don't shoot," yelled the black male.

36

Shaffer

Despite all the commotion, Shaffer was poised, using his instincts as a detective. Station Street was blocked off with a fire truck, paramedics, and crime scene technicians collecting evidence. The scene of the accident was a few feet from the shooting. Moore arrested Will, handcuffing him and placing him in the backseat of the unmarked vehicle. Shaffer walked down the sidewalk, shining his flashlight on the ground and searching for clues. There were several cars parked on the street, and neighbors stood outside, some on the sidewalks and some on their porches.

"It's a bunch of kids having a party over there," said one of the neighbors. "They shot the house up." Shaffer shined his light towards the home and noticed the house was riddled with bullet holes.

When he approached the steps, he shined his flashlight back and forth, his eyebrows raised at the amount of damage. He took a deep breath and exhaled while walking up the steps, gun and flashlight in hand, not knowing what to expect when he entered. He opened the wooden door, which was also filled with bullet holes, and stepped on broken pieces of glass on the floor.

Rubbing his hand across the wall to his left, he felt for a light switch and flipped the switch up.

He saw several bodies lying on the floor.

"We need emergency medic units at 456 South Greenwood, "he said, speaking into his mic. "Several people have been shot."

Some of the teens were moaning, and some were lying on the floor, unresponsive. He went to take a step towards them, but froze with his eyes wide open as he gazed across the living room. Fear overwhelmed his spirit, and his heart dropped to the floor and shattered like a glass.

No. It can't be, he thought. There was a teenage girl lying face down, motionless, with long brown hair that resembled Riley's. Her body was parallel to a tan sofa, her head directly in front of a TV stand. *She's home,* he thought numbly.

The detective stepped over Jerome, who was the first body, without checking his pulse, not remembering him from the night of the basketball game. Jerome was lying in a pool of blood, but Shaffer wanted to get a closer look at the girl.

The first thing he noticed was the gunshot wound on the upper right side of her back, and her baby blue sweatshirt soaked with blood. Then he noticed her earrings.

His heart dropped.

37

Jerome 4

Jerome woke groggily after four hours of surgery. His vision was blurry, and his mind was foggy.

"Ma," he called, looking around the room, frightened from the trauma of the shooting. He tried to move, but his left wrist was handcuffed to the bedrail. His shoulder was wrapped in large white gauze. One of the bullets had entered his side and came out of his upper right shoulder. His side was bandaged, and his right leg had a large cast on it. There were tubes in his nose to help him breath, and he had an IV in his right arm.

When he looked around, he saw a detective at his bedside. The man wore a gray polo golf shirt, black slacks, black shoes, and carried a gun on the right side of his waist. Jerome's mother sat with her legs crossed in a chair on the opposite side.

An attorney stood next to her.

He was tall and must have weighed 250 pounds. He had a buzz cut and perched a pair of tan Ray-Bans on his head. He wore a gray three-piece suit, with a red tie and a black trench coat. A shiny black leather brief case sat on the floor.

Detective Moore read Jerome his rights, and the attorney agreed to allow the detectives to question him.

"I will tell you what questions not to answer, Jerome," said the attorney.

"Ma? What's going on?" Jerome asked, his voice cracking.

"There was a shooting, baby. You and some of your friends were hurt," Velma said, tearing up.

Jerome still didn't understand, and it must have showed, because Detective Moore, the attorney, and Velma all glanced at one another.

"Do you remember anything that happened last night?" Moore asked.

"I remember Riley came over. I remember talking to her. I opened the door for Omar," he said, frowning. There was moment of silence as he tried to recollect. "And there was some dudes. They were standing outside a car." He lifted his arm and stared at the cuff. "Why am I handcuffed?" he asked. "And where is Riley?"

"Who were the guys you saw?" Moore asked.

"I don't know, but they had guns," said Jerome. "Where's Riley," he repeated, yanking his left arm as if he could break the cuff.

"Jerome, calm down," Ma pleaded. "Please answer the detective's questions."

"What happened after you opened the door for Omar?" Moore asked.

"The dudes started shooting," he said.

"Did anyone in the house return fire?" Moore asked.

"I don't know. I dove on the floor. I tried to grab Riley. I don't remember anything else."

"There was a gun in your closet," Moore said. "A black nine-millimeter. How long have you had it?"

"I found it in the garbage," Jerome answered.

"Boy, you know I don't want no guns in my house," said Velma, waving her fingers in his direction.

"What garbage did you find the gun in?" asked Moore, taking notes in his notepad.

"I took the garbage out. It was in there," he replied.

"That gun was used in a homicide a few days ago. Your prints are the only prints on it," Moore explained. "Do you know who put it there?"

Jerome closed his eyes. He envisioned Omar walking briskly through the field and across the street, shortly after hearing the gunfire that night. "I don't know," he replied.

"Can you give me a moment with my son, sir?" Velma asked, pursing her lips in disbelief.

"Sure." Moore put his pen in his pocket and stepped out of the room.

Velma rose to her feet, enraged. "Omar put that gun there, didn't he?" she asked. She stared her son down, holding on to the bed rail as she did.

Jerome cut his eyes away from his mom and shrugged.

"I know when you're lying, Jerome. You need to tell that man who put that gun there. They're trying to pin that murder on you, fool."

"Murder?" he asked, blinking rapidly.

"Yes, *murder*. You should've listened to me when I told you the first time. To *stay away* from that boy," she stressed, glaring at him.

Jerome shook his head. "I ain't no snitch."

"A snitch? This is your *life*, Jerome. You've worked so hard and you're about to throw it all away," she cried. "For what? To protect a murderer?" She threw her arms up.

Jerome laid back in the bed in silence. He knew Ma was right, but he didn't want his friend to know he told.

"Your mother's right, Jerome," said the attorney. "A first degree murder charge in Illinois carries a minimum of twenty years in prison."

"Someone's son died. You said you knew that boy from school. His mother is in pain. Do what's right," Velma pleaded.

Jerome was in tears. Although he didn't know for sure that Omar killed Timmy, he was almost certain. "Okay," he said. "I'll talk."

The lawyer opened the door, and Detective Moore came back in the room.

"Jerome, tell the detective what you know."

The teenager took a deep breath. "The night Timmy died, I was sitting on the porch and I saw Omar arguing with his ma out front. Omar started walking down Greenwood dressed in all black. I went to bed around ten; I text my ma that night before I went to sleep. Then I woke up to gunshots. A few minutes later, I looked out my window and saw Omar walking across the field, fast. He was watching his back like somebody was after him. The next day I took out the trash, and that's when I found the gun. Omar put it there."

Detective Moore tapped his pen on his notepad. "I believe you, son, but unless Omar confesses, there's nothing that links him to that gun."

"What? He told you everything," Velma protested.

"Jerome's prints are all over the murder weapon, ma'am," said Detective Moore. "What about tonight?"

"Omar was there tonight, too," Jerome added. "He was busting back at the dudes in the street."

"Do you have any idea where Omar could be?" the detective asked.

Jerome thought for a second, looking up at the ceiling. "He's probably down the street at Perry's crib."

38

Omar 2

Omar disappeared into the night air with no trace of him but shell casings, and a gun in Jerome's bedroom that had no physical connection to him.

He sprinted to Perry's crib, the gun still hot in his palm, his heart racing. He prayed to himself along the way and watched his back obsessively until he reached the back door of Perry's.

Omar knocked on the door harder and faster as the emergency lights flashed in the night sky and the sirens drew closer to him. Perry answered the door, ready to yell at whoever was on the other end, but calmed his nerves after seeing the gun in Omar's palm.

"Damn, what happened?" Perry asked as he canvassed the yard.

"Let me in bro," Omar said, breathing hard from the run.

They went downstairs to the basement, and Omar sat on an old green couch with a coffee table in front of it. The coffee table contained a pile of weed and about five swishers next to it. Omar told him what happened and asked him to get rid of the heat.

Perry tossed him a white towel from the laundry basket, and Omar wiped it clean and placed it on the table. Perry sat next to him and observed Omar, who was a nervous wreck; biting his fingernails and flinching at the headlights glaring through the basement windows.

"You bout to roll up?" Omar asked, fidgeting.

"Hell yeah, cuz you a nervous wreck my nigga," Perry answered. Perry split a blunt down the middle with a razor and sprinkled weed in it. In the middle of their smoke session, Perry decided to put his lawyer cap on and give Omar some legal advice.

"That was self-defense, bro. You may do time for the pistol, but you don't got no felonies. You'll probably get probation or some shit."

Omar was still shaken, but he felt more at ease while talking to Perry.

"You think ole boy gonna talk?" asked Perry, referring to Jerome.

"I don't know. He a lame though. He bout to go to college," said Omar, passing the blunt to Perry.

"Shit. I wish I was a lame. That nigga must be Einstein or something, going to Harvard." Perry blew the smoke out and passed it back. "This street life ain't no joke."

Omar took the blunt from Perry, and sucked the smoke into his lungs. He held it for few seconds, exhaled, then dropped it to the floor after hearing a loud boom at the back door.

"Police!"

39

Riley 2

Riley was somewhat coherent as her father applied pressure to the gunshot wound on the upper right side of her back. She could hear him, but she could not respond.

"Stay with me, baby," he said, sounding muffled, as if she had water in her ears after going for a swim. She struggled to breathe, and the fear of dying made her want to weep.

I don't want to die, she thought, squeezing her father's hand tighter and tighter the more she struggled to breathe.

I should have listened to you, Daddy, she said internally, regretting her decision to go to the party. In her darkest moment, she wondered where Jerome was and why he wasn't with her when she needed him most. *Is he hurt too?* she wondered, her eyes moving back and forth. She could hear the sirens from outside, and the flashing lights kept her awake as the emergency medical personnel entered the home.

"Don't let her die," her father yelled. "Do you hear me? Don't let her die," he repeated, following them out of the home.

The fear of dying was somewhat relieved after an oxygen mask was placed over her mouth and nose, making it easier to breath. *Everything's going to be okay,* she thought. *I'm going to make it, Daddy.*

The ride in the ambulance was all of three minutes, but by the time the paramedics rushed her into the triage, Riley was unconscious, her pulse low and fading fast. Her last conscious thought was wondering where her mom was.

The doctor did thirty chest compressions, but before he could open her airway, Riley flat-lined. He grabbed the defibrillators and shocked her twice.

The line stayed flat.

He repeated the shocks again, but he got the same results. "She's gone," he said, dropping the defibrillators in disappointment.

The nurse covered Riley's lifeless body, and the doctor took his gloves off with frustration. The physician was filled with resentment as he walked out to the waiting room to tell Riley's parents that their daughter was dead.

40

Lynn 2

Lynn was sickened as paramedics wheeled in body after a body on stretchers at Riverside. She asked one of the medics what happened.

"A shootout on South Greenwood in Kankakee," the medic replied. "There were a lot more, but some of them were taken down the road to St. Mary's."

The worry she felt began to distract her from the lives she needed to save in the moment. There was only one life she could think of.

Riley's.

Why hadn't she gotten the address of the party from her daughter? Why didn't she know where that boy lived, so she would know where her daughter was and if she was safe?

Lynn's cell phone was in her locker, so she had no way to contact her. She stood in on an emergency surgery procedure for one of the teens who had non-life-threatening injuries. Another nurse came in to relieve her early, which puzzled her until the nurse told her why.

She had a phone call that she needed to take.

Lynn rushed out of the room and to the desk in the triage to take her call. Her heart raced faster than it ever had. *Not my princess*, she thought. She picked up the phone. It was her husband.

"Come to St. Mary's," he said curtly. "Now."

Lynn sped down Court Street, wishing she could redo her phone call with Riley. She wished she could've said something to stop her. "Why did you let her go?" she asked. She didn't know who she meant; herself. Her husband. God. "Heavenly Father, please. Not her!"

She drove through the main entrance at St. Mary's and jumped out of the car so quickly that she left the keys in the ignition. She ran through the parking lot and into the emergency waiting room where her husband paced back and forth and prayed to the heavens above.

She was there for less than a minute when the doctor walked out. She could tell by the look on his face that it wasn't good.

The energy in the room was cold, and the pretense of death touched the depths of her soul. When the doctor informed them of Riley's passing, she went into a trance, as if she was stuck in the twilight zone. She buried her face into her husband's chest and screamed a scream that only a mother could roar.

But her cries were much deeper than what could be externally visualized or heard by the human ear. The guilt of supporting Riley's decision to attend the party pierced her heart, as if God brought Cupid's blackened arrow to life.

How could she tell her husband? How could she tell him that she let Riley go? He'd hate her forever.

But not as much as she hated herself.

41

Brenda 2

Brenda stood outside amongst all the commotion, looking back and forth for Omar, but he was nowhere in sight. She called his phone repeatedly.

"Come on, Omar. Answer the phone," she pleaded, but he did not answer. Worry resided in the pit of her stomach, growing each time the greeting message on his voice mail picked up.

"It's Big O, leave it."

She had no idea where he was. On top of it, she was worried about Jerome, too, after seeing him carried down the steps on a stretcher. *Maybe he's at the hospital,* she thought. Although she didn't have a valid reason to believe Omar was there, a dreadful feeling came over here nonetheless.

She drove to St. Mary's in fear that Omar could be amongst the teens being treated. When she entered the crowded emergency room, she was stunned by the amount of people loitering in the waiting room. The sadness and worry upon their faces caused her to freeze. She seemed lost, so a security guard approached her to be of some assistance.

"Can I help you, ma'am?" he asked.

His words awakened her from the brief daydream, causing her to flinch. "No, thank you," she said, combing the side of hair back with her fingers. She approached the information desk, fidgeting and breathing deeply before speaking to the ER receptionist. "There was a shooting tonight, and, and I can't find my son. His name is Omar Flowers. Is he here?" she asked.

254

The receptionist said, "One moment," and walked back towards the triage. Brenda waited impatiently until the receptionist returned what felt like an eternity later, but was probably only a few minutes.

"We don't have anyone here by that name. Did you try Riverside?"

"No, but thanks," said Brenda, visibly shaken.

She made an attempt to walk out the automatic sliding doors, but someone called her name. She stopped and turned around.

It was Velma, Jerome's mother. Her eyes were swollen and red, and Brenda could tell she'd been crying. She also looked furious.

"Where's Omar?" asked Velma, tears building in her eyes, threatening to spill her pain.

"I don't know, I'm looking for him and he won't answer the phone," cried Brenda. "Is Jerome okay?"

"He's going to pull through, but you're not going to find Omar because he's on the run."

"On the run," Brenda repeated with confusion, rubbing her chin.

"Yes. On the run. He's the cause of all this commotion, and now my baby is being *charged with murder*," Velma said angrily.

"What are you talking about?" Brenda asked.

"Damn girl! You don't know what your child been doing? Omar killed Sharon's boy," Velma yelled. "That's what this whole mess is over!"

Brenda began to swallow excessively, her gaze shooting downward to hide her shame. Everyone in the waiting room area became silent and directed their attention towards the heated exchange. Brenda mulled over the night Omar came home suspiciously after she heard gunshots.

"Nothing to say, huh?" Velma asked, her voice quivering with emotion. "If you spent more time raising him instead of drinking yourself to death, Jerome wouldn't be handcuffed to a bed."

Velma's words spewed from her heart furiously as she walked in Brenda's direction with rage gripping her, her blood as hot as an Arizona summer. The security guard responded quickly, standing in between them after observing Velma's intent to do harm.

Brenda ran out of the sliding doors, hoping to find Omar at Riverside Hospital. Before she could put the car in reverse, though, her phone rang.

It was an unknown number.

She accepted the call nervously, preparing herself to hear that Omar was dead.

"Hello," she answered, her voice trembling.

"This is Detective Moore with the Kankakee County Police Department. May I speak with Brenda Flowers, please?"

There was a tightening in her throat, and streams of tears flowed from her eyes like a river.

"This is she," said Brenda.

"We have your son, Omar Flowers, at the station. We need to question him, but since he's a minor, we cannot proceed without you or a lawyer being present," said Detective Moore.

"What is he being charged with?"

"We will discuss the details when you're here," the detective replied.

"I'm on my way." Brenda ended the call. She wailed loudly, "God, no!"

42

<u>Chloe 2</u>

Chloe clocked out after working a five-hour shift at Arby's, somewhat down after Kelly shunned her. She'd been texting Riley off and on throughout her shift, with plans to go to Jerome's party with or without Kelly. Riley told her how her parents had forbid her from going to Kankakee, and although she still planned on going, feared going alone. "Kankakee? Are you sure? A dude got murdered there a few days ago," Chloe said.

"I know, and my dad is freaking out. Not only does he not want me anywhere near K3, he doesn't want me to have a black boyfriend," Riley lamented. "He said we all should be with our own kind."

"Our own kind," Chloe snorted. "What does that even mean? Our parents are so stupid. Who cares what color someone is as long as they're a good person? That's all that should matter."

After hearing why Riley's parents didn't want her to go, Chloe felt obligated to support her friend. Except Riley wanted to pick her up by ten.

"You're kidding, right? I don't get off work until nine, and then I have to walk home. That will leave me thirty minutes to get ready."

"C'mon Chloe, just throw something on. I'm wearing Jerome's hoodie and some jeans. I promise we won't be there long," she said.

She sighed. "I guess. I can do my makeup in the car, and I'll wear a hoodie, too."

Chloe's parents had gone to a wedding, so she had to walk home, which frustrated her because of the rainfall. Nevertheless, she put her work cap on and walked down North Street. It was a quarter after nine when she crossed the train tracks. There was an eerie silence in the air. The streets were empty and lightning flashed every so often. Chloe walked quickly down Washington when a pair of bright headlights flashed from behind her. She turned her head while covering her eyes from the glare.

She picked up the pace as a van strolled by slowly, but she couldn't see who the driver was. She made a right on Hemlock, and so did the van, stopping where she'd crossed the street.

"Is that you, Riley?" she asked, walking cautiously towards the middle of the street. Had she borrowed a friend's car?

Suddenly the driver's side door opened, and she observed a dark figure rushing towards her, swinging an unidentified object.

Everything went black.

When Chloe woke up, she couldn't see.

It took her a moment to realize that she had been blindfolded. Her mouth was duct taped shut, and her wrists and ankles were bound together. She'd been stripped down to her panties. It was pitch black, and she had no idea where she was or how she'd gotten there. She was overwhelmed with horrifying fear, and started wailing after hearing a set of keys rattle.

Moments later the blindfold was ripped off and she saw a man. A man she did not know. She tried to scream, but couldn't.

"Hi, neighbor," he said. "It's nice to finally meet you." He rubbed his fingers through her hair, then stroked the side of her face. "I know your name is Chloe. My name is Fred," he said.

Chloe's thoughts were filled with regret as Fred began to violate her, touching her in private areas of her body with his rough hands. She whimpered as she began to reflect on a conversation she had with her step father a week prior.

Chloe hated her stepdad Bruce, mainly because he wasn't her real dad. Her mother divorced her biological father, and she blamed Bruce for it. Bruce did all he could to bond with Chloe, but she remained distant, only talking to him when she had to. But there were times he tried his best to offer guidance.

He had knocked on her bedroom door that evening. Chloe was lying across her bed, on the phone with Riley, and she yelled "Come in" after a huge sigh.

Bruce had walked into the bedroom, dressed in his blue jump suit for his graveyard shift at the Nucor steel company. Chloe placed Riley on hold, then sat cross-legged on the bed, with her head down to avoid eye contact.

He told her about the new Snapchat feature he'd seen on the news. A man tracked his cheating girlfriend down using the Snap map feature, and when he arrived at the location, he found her with her lover. He stabbed the man to the death. The news reporter walked viewers through the Snapchat settings, showing them how to disable the feature.

Bruce advised her to disable the feature, out of fear of what could happen.

Chloe remembered saying, "I know, but I only have my friends on my Snap."

"Look. I know you blame me for everything, but I'm just trying to keep you safe," he said.

Chloe said okay to appease him, then picked up the phone to resume her conversation. Bruce shook his head and left the bedroom, his shoulders slumped.

Chloe was a free-spirited girl who saw the best in everyone. She didn't believe the world was as crazy as everyone made it seem.

"Why are adults so paranoid?" she had asked Riley. "They always assume the worst is going to happen. Bruce wants me to disable my location on Snapchat. He's afraid the boogie man is going to get me," she laughed.

It was no longer a laughing matter.

Chloe tried to scream again, but she couldn't. Her moans and groans were faint, and went unheard in the dark, secluded area.

"You can stop trying to scream. No one can hear you out here," Fred said. Chloe watched as the man disrobed himself, and she finally realized the truth.

The boogie man had gotten her.

43

Shaffer 2

Velma sped through traffic to meet the detective at the
hospital where Jerome was still hospitalized, but in
police custody. She had no idea what she was walking
into, but she hoped it was good news.

Her eyes were swollen from crying and from a
sleepless night; her mind couldn't rest until everything
was settled. When she arrived, her hope turned into
suspicion after seeing Detective Moore and Detective
Shaffer waiting for her in the lobby of the main entrance.
She could tell Shaffer was upset, but she didn't know

why. They walked together to the ICU, where Jerome was still recovering from his surgery.

Jerome was watching Judge Judy when they entered the room, and turned the television off immediately. He was a bit disturbed by Shaffer's presence, and wondered why he was there.

"Hey, Ma," he said, smiling nervously. "Did you get some rest?" he asked.

"Not at all," she answered, slowly taking a seat in the chair next to his bed. "Have you heard anything about Riley?" he asked.

The two detectives remained standing. Moore offered a smile, which comforted both Jerome and Velma. Shaffer stood as stiff as a board, staring at the floor, as if he was deep in thought.

"We have some good news," Moore said, adjusting his blue tie. "Omar Flowers confessed to the murder of Timothy Gray. The charges against you have been dropped."

Both Jerome and Velma smiled big. She rose from the chair and kissed her son repeatedly on his forehead and cheeks. "Thank you, Jesus," she said.

"William Gray was arrested at the scene and charged with attempted murder and murder in the first degree for the shooting last night," Moore continued. "One of the other perpetrators, Ja' Corey Tucker, is deceased."

A call came in on the detectives' scanner, disrupting the conversation. The dispatcher alerted them to two bodies found in a Dollar Tree parking lot. "...possible overdose, one male deceased, one female alive but unresponsive," the dispatcher concluded.

"I got it," Moore said. He left the room, but not before giving his partner a pat on the back, his face somber. Shaffer stayed, approaching Jerome's bedside with keys in his hand and tears in his eyes. Jerome watched him, clueless as to why Shaffer had all of a sudden become emotional.

He took the cuff off Jerome and held it in his hands while staring the teen in his eyes. "I hear you're going to Harvard," he said, swiping at his eyes to catch the tears. "Riley said you were different, and to be honest, I didn't believe her."

Jerome was puzzled momentarily, but realized where he knew Shaffer from after recollecting on the night of the basketball game. "You're Riley's dad? How is she?" Jerome asked him. "Is she here?"

Shaffer disregarded his question, and continued speaking his piece, his face turning red. "I want to hate you so bad, but I can't. You were just as innocent as her, and now that she's gone, I owe it to her to tell you that I'm sorry," he said. He began to cry.

"She's gone," Jerome repeated numbly, tears in his eyes.

Velma sat speechless as she dried her eyes with a napkin she found in her purse.

"My baby girl is gone," Shaffer said his head down. He buried his face in his hands.

44

Dontae & Gloria

Dontae woke up the next day, and the first thing he did was check his newsfeed on Facebook. There was post after post about the shooting: Tierra posted, *"No more juke parties for me. I caught one in the leg, but thank God I'm still here."* Kyla made a post, *"At a loss for words. Now my kids have to grow up without their uncle and their father Smh."* He was flabbergasted by the amount of RIP posts, and even more stunned after discovering that Will and Corey were behind the shooting. He removed his blanket and raced down the stairs barefoot and shirtless, with only navy blue pajama pants on, to the kitchen where Gloria was.

"Ma!" he yelled.

"Boy, it is too early for you to be calling my name."

"Did you hear about what happened last night?" he asked, taking a seat at the kitchen table next to her, putting his phone in her face.

Gloria had a white coffee mug in her hand with the words "Live, Laugh, Love" on it. She'd just taken a sip. "Yep, I know what happened," she said, looking at the phone.

"Will called me last night and tried to get me to go with them," he admitted.

"Hmm, and what did you say?" Gloria asked.

"I told him I never shot a gun before, and that you're watching me like a hawk," he said.

"You could've been in that car with them. Dead or in jail," Gloria said, shaking her head. "See what happens when you listen?"

Dedication

To my daughter, Sa' Mareah Thompson, Thanks for not only motivating me to write this book, but for also being one of my biggest inspirations. I love you

Other books by La' Kendrick Thompson

- Black in America: The Life and Times of Tank Thompson (Volume 1)
- Black in America: The Life and Times of Tank Thompson (Volume 2)
- The Truth About Candy

Coming Soon

- The Color of Love (TBA)
- Mood: Venting through Poetry (TBA)